I: (ONE)

WAR OF ROSES BOOK 3

LANA SKY

I

I: (One)

I: (One) By Lana Sky

ISBN: 978-1-956608-05-2

ACKNOWLEDGMENTS

Mickey, thank you so very much for taking the time to help me perfect this draft. As always, your feedback and expertise have been invaluable. Thank you, Charity for applying the final touches on this draft.

Thanks so much to everyone who supported this draft along the way, including the many beta readers who provided encouragement along the way! Please keep in mind that this story includes dark, graphic and explicit content matter that is not suitable for readers under the age of 18—or for readers who are uncomfortable with the following subject matter: explicit sex, mentions of sexual abuse, and graphic depictions of violence.

PREFACE

My mother defined hell as a rose. One, she mused, with all the life sucked out of it. Its thorns had become knives, and the leaves swallowed up the stalk. Even so, underneath the violence, it was still beautiful.

I used to believe that philosophy was her subtle attempt at religion. But now, years later, I know what she truly meant.

Hopeless damnation isn't contained in a realm of fire and brimstone—but somewhere far more dangerous. It springs from your soul, growing on creeping vines, and claims your heart before you realize it.

In my mother's view, the worst torture couldn't be felt through pain, or death, or silence.

To her, hell was love—and it was every bit as insidious as a corrupted rose.

CHAPTER 1

Mischa Stepanov has brutalized my body in ways I could have never imagined. My face bears his permanent mark, and he made me sever my own ring finger to feed his lie. He's toyed with me. Mocked me.

But this is the cruelest torture he's inflicted. His aim isn't to merely hurt me.

He's after my soul.

And his attack comes in the form of one sentence only he could deliver.

"I can help you find your son."

Even though Sergei Vasilev is standing before me, I know who's responsible for this. And I know that only lies lurk in the envelope brandished in his outstretched hand.

That's all this is: lies.

It *has* to be.

"You don't believe me?" Sergei's mouth twists into a contemplative frown. When I don't move, he raises the envelope higher, letting the ivory surface catch the dim light in the hall. "Fine. I'll say it again: I have proof that your son is still alive—"

"Please don't do this." I sound so hollow. Not angry. Not panicked. Just so damn tired. When he takes a step forward, I throw out my hand as if my trembling palm alone can ward him off. At least, for now, it does. "Please…"

"No?" A low hiss rumbles from his throat. A sigh? "I must admit that I expected you to receive this news differently."

"Did Mischa tell you?" I stare at my hands. The fingers twitch, aching to guard my ears against any more lies. "About my…*him*?"

"Mischa?" The inflection in his tone is convincing. He sounds confused—but I've already decided.

Only a man like Mischa would weaponize my darkest secrets against me. In fact, he'd relish in doing so.

"Well, he lied to you." I force a weak laugh as I scan the hall for my tormentor. Is he lurking there beyond the stairwell? Or maybe around the corner?

No matter the hiding place, he's somewhere close, savoring his victory.

"Mischa didn't tell me a thing." Sergei sounds too damn genuine. Smug, almost. He knows my captor better than I do.

"He's the only one I've told," I confess, hating myself for being so foolish. "No one else."

"Is that so?" Sergei surprises me by throwing his head back, and of all things, he…laughs. "Child, I've known about your son since the day he was born." When he meets my gaze, there is no amusement in his expression. Just unsettling insight that betrays a knowledge of so much more than I'm willing to accept. "In fact, I've known about *you* since the day you were born."

"How?"

I hunt his wizened features for any hint of a lie and come to one grim observation: He shields his emotions well. Better than Mischa. It's as if he can flick a switch, displaying only what he chooses to. And in this moment? His eyes reveal nothing.

"Your husband has hidden him well, your son," he says softly. "So well that my spies have gotten only a glimpse of him in four years—"

"How can I believe you?"

"You don't have to." He nods to the envelope. "You merely need to see for yourself."

He steps forward cautiously, giving me plenty of time to back away. When he's close enough, he presses the envelope into my hand and coaxes my fingers into curling over the square surface.

"I am the only one who can help you rescue him—"

"And Mischa can't?" Through watering, burning eyes, I watch his expression flicker—the briefest hint of irritation.

"Mischa rescue the son of his sworn enemy?" His doubtful tone reveals what he thinks of that scenario. "You and I both know that he could sooner chop the boy into pieces and sell him off to the highest bidder—"

"And you wouldn't?" God only knows why I'm even playing this game. The envelope in my fist burns. Every cell in my body warns me to let it go. I watch my nails flex over it, but the damn thing won't fall. Looking up, I meet Sergei's gaze directly. "Why would you even want to help me?"

"Because you are blood." His eyes flash, reinforcing the heat in his tone. "*He* is my blood."

Tears finally escape, obscuring my vision. When Sergei brushes his hand across my cheek, I can't even tell if the act contains genuine emotion or not.

"I want to teach you," he says. "You deserve a seat at the table, as my heir—"

"Your time is up, Sergei."

I stiffen at the sound of Mischa's voice.

He lurks near the mouth of the hall, paces away. When he spots Sergei's hand on my face, his eyes become slits. "I upheld my end of the bargain. Now, you can leave."

"I'll continue to provide my support," Sergei promises and he steps back—out of respect, not fear. "And if I'm needed, my men will know how to contact me. Goodnight."

I watch him push past me, toward the front of the cottage. His steps echo, slow and heavy, as if he expects me to take him up on his implied offer any minute.

But I remain silent, the perfect prey for Mischa to pounce on. His hand slams against the wall inches from my face, trapping me in place as he corners me from behind.

"Don't tell me," he murmurs into my ear. "I missed all the fun, didn't I—"

I push away from him and lunge for the stairs. Every step is a struggle, and by the time I reach the landing, I'm forced to hobble into the nearest room and slam the door behind me. Then I lean against it for good measure.

This small room contains only a bed and a rickety wooden chair in a corner—there's nothing to hide behind. I have no defense against the attack that I know is coming.

Sure enough, heavy footsteps rattle the floorboards in my wake.

"What did he say?" Mischa demands harshly through the door. He tests the handle once but doesn't push the door open. Yet. "What did he say?"

Closing my eyes, I try to ignore him—ignore everything. My psyche is a fractured mirror, and for so damn long, I've carefully hoarded the pieces, holding them in place with sheer determination.

Breathe…

Breathe…

"Fine, Rose. Play your little game of silence."

The walls themselves seem to sigh as Mischa retreats down the steps. He's angry. I'll pay for this later in the form of some insult or another.

I don't care.

His absence depletes my body of any ounce of fight and I slide to my knees. Through blurred vision, I scan the surface of Sergei's envelope. There are no markings on it. No hint as to its contents. My clenching fingers strain the thin parchment to the point of tearing it.

Then I throw it so hard that it bounces off the opposite wall.

"Ellen?"

Footsteps creep toward my door again. Not Mischa's, but someone slower, his pace uneven.

"It's me," Vanya says and I stiffen. Mischa probably sent him, utilizing another to do his dirty work. "Are you all right?"

"I'm…" In my mind, I envision those shattered pieces that make up who I am. To hold them together, I need to lie. Push back all remnants of the past. Suppress. Repress. Ignore. Ignore. Ignore.

I attempt to, but the pieces shatter further, and I can't protect myself from the aftermath.

"You knew Marnie Winthorp," I croak.

He's silent for so damn long. I try to imagine his expression, but I can't. He is an enigma, so different from the callous men I'm used to. Unlike them, Vanya has yet to lie to my face, or hit me, or deceive.

Which makes him more dangerous than a thousand Mischas combined. He's earned my trust on his own merit.

I can only hope I've earned his honesty.

"Did you?" I press to break the silence.

"Yes," he finally admits. His voice is so hollow that I barely recognize it. "I knew her."

"H-how?" Those vicious scenarios Mischa posed creep into my thoughts. *Brutalized. Kidnapped. Raped.*

I squeeze my eyes shut, desperate to fight the onslaught that I know is coming. But it's too late. More tears creep beneath my eyelids and spill down my cheeks in spite.

"You're crying." A gentle thud rattles the door as if he braced his hand against it from the other end. "Ellen…"

"Did you hurt her?" I ask, choking my sobs down. I can't seem to breathe again until his heavy sigh slips through the crack in the doorway.

"Never," he swears. "I would have never hurt her—"

"Did you hate her? She was your enemy," I point out. Before he can reply, I add, "Did…did you love her?"

Seconds of silence trickle into minutes.

"Tell me about her," I demand, changing tack again. "Please."

"She was brave," he says haltingly. "So damn brave. You wouldn't expect it, coming from a tiny thing like that. She was beautiful too…" The door bows against my back as if he's leaning against it from the other end. "So damn beautiful. I would never hurt her."

"But you kidnapped her," I insist. "Or your brother did, or…" I bury my face in my hands, digging my fingers into my temples. "It doesn't matter. You took her and then she escaped. But how? Why?" It takes everything I have to bite back the most important question of all.

Why did you abandon me?

"I don't know what you've been told," Vanya says, as gentle as always. "Some of it, admittedly, might be true. But some…" He sighs again and the wood creaks, protesting against more pressure exuded on it from the other side. I wonder if the damn thing will give way altogether. He'll break through.

Just as the hinges start to squeal, the pressure recedes and the wood jarringly snaps back into place.

"Just know this," he says thickly. "She was never my captive. Not for one second. And she didn't escape. I let her go—" His voice breaks, but he grunts, regaining his composure. "I let *her* go. Goodnight."

"Wait." I scramble to my knees and reach for the doorknob —but he's already gone and my eyes continue to overflow.

No man on Earth could fake the pain in his voice—or the raw honesty, either.

No matter the circumstances of their relationship, I don't doubt that he let Marnie go.

Or that *she* went back to Robert Winthorp, Sr. of her own accord.

Which means…*she* let me live as her dirty, unwanted secret.

And maybe most telling of all…

If Sergei wasn't lying, then she never even told my father about *me.*

CHAPTER 2

It feels like hours pass before I finally gather up the strength to stand and cross over to that crumpled envelope. I lift it carefully from the floor and wipe away the dust and grime newly coating that mocking white. Then I shove it beneath the bed's lumpy mattress and turn away, pushing it from my mind altogether.

Maybe I just don't have the heart to rip it into pieces like I should.

Or perhaps I just need it to serve one pathetic purpose: proof. Unlike Marnie Winthorp, I refuse to be used as a pawn, shuffled between players on the gameboard. From now on, I can only act on what I know. What I feel in my bones.

My past must stay dead.

I can't be manipulated again.

And it feels so damn good to leave that room, knowing that the only person driving my actions is me. Even as I sway unsteadily on trembling legs—at least I'm no longer Marnie's naïve mistake or Mischa's unwilling victim.

But as I wander the rickety hall beyond the staircase, I'm forced to admit one reality: I'm still a mouse trapped in a maze.

At least I'm not the only creature forced to jump through the hoops of this new world. Not far from the other room, I come across the one the little girl's lying in. My fellow Mouse, in the literal sense. Despite the late hour, she's sitting upright in bed, staring intently as a hulking figure attempts to spread jam on a piece of toast.

"Too much or not enough?" he gruffly inquires, holding his slathered slice up for input.

Unsatisfied, Mouse wrinkles her nose and shakes her head in a silent command. *More.*

"Fine." Sighing, Mischa applies another layer of jam. "Do you know how much sugar is in this shit? You're going to be bouncing off the walls—"

I must have made a sound, because he turns, breaking off. Oddly enough, my presence is acknowledged with only a grunt before he returns his attention to the girl.

"The old man says you can start walking around tomorrow," he continues, presumably referring to Vanya. "But I don't know… All this sugary shit and you might be able to *fly*."

He relinquishes the slice of bread, which the girl promptly shoves into her mouth.

Looking at him, she cuts her eyes in my direction and Mischa copies her. Then he laughs.

"You watch your mouth," he scolds, running his palm over her scalp. "It's rude to call people names."

"And what is that?" I ask, stepping over the threshold.

Both figures turn to me and share another mischievous look.

"That's it," Mischa declares. My cheeks prickle with heat as he throws his head back and laughs more genuinely than I think I've ever heard. "Bedtime." He snatches the tray of bread and jam and places it on a table beyond her reach. "No more sweet stuff for you. You get too mouthy." He looks at me, still smirking, and my heart lurches.

Strip him of anger and he can appear human.

But like this?

He's a different man, glimpsed through the window of a rare second when he has no guard to maintain or façade to uphold.

But just as quickly, the hardened criminal returns and his smile transforms into a seething glare.

"I'll be back," he barks to Mouse before advancing on my position. "But first, Little Rose and I need to have a chat—"

I turn before he can finish and lead the way back to the room I came from while he follows. Rage lashes from him like a weapon. It slices at my skin, fighting to leave a mark —but my new armor is impenetrable, it seems: I've just stopped caring.

"What did he say to you?" Mischa demands as he barrels into the room, slamming the door. The violent thud echoes like a gunshot—and all I can do is laugh in its terrifying wake. "Something funny, I'm guessing?" He grabs my arm, wrenching me around to face him. "Did you two come up with some hilarious little scheme to—"

"Kiss me."

"What?" He blinks, his words ending in a shocked grunt.

I've startled him so greatly that he loosened his grip, but I don't capitalize on my new freedom. I endure him. Desperate, my nostrils flare for his scent and I choke it down with every breath—it's the only way to keep the dark memories Sergei unearthed at bay.

By dancing with another devil.

"Kiss me." I tilt my head back to meet his gaze fully, watching rage go to war with confusion. "Do it," I add. "Or was all that talk about wanting me just that? Talk—"

"Fine." He reclaims my shoulders, yanking me forward.

Our lips meet fiercely—teeth on flesh. Nipping. Tearing. Bruising.

But *I'm* the one doing the most damage. Like this, I can't think. He demands my sole attention, grinding his presence into my skin, forcing me to react. Breathe. Feel. There is no room for doubt, or pain, or anything else.

Just Mischa.

Luckily, consuming me is one task he doesn't hesitate to fulfill. His hands rake through my hair, teasing out any thoughts that don't contain him as he backs me toward the bed. Shoves me onto it. While I fight to catch my breath, he grabs my thighs, spreading them apart as his fingers come to tease me open.

"Look at me."

He's still fuming. Our conversation isn't finished yet—but he draws it out nonverbally instead. A searching thumb shoved inside me contains a futile plea he won't ever voice out loud: *How can I trust you?* Brutally, he repeats that refrain, thrusting inside me over and over as my toes curl. *How? How? How?*

All I can do is relax into the violence and compile my own primal answer. How can he trust me?

By letting me in. My tongue at first, sliding along his lower lip. Then my hands, sinking through his hair. Gradually, he removes his thumb from inside me and replaces it with something larger—and presents a more pressing question.

Can you ever trust me?

My body isn't sure at first. Tension seizes my muscles, paralyzing me. He's too fucking big—and though I've already taken him multiple times, this moment feels different.

The thin mattress is unforgiving. There's no resistance to each shallow thrust of his hips as tender flesh molds to his shape like clay. When he finally moves inside me, he goes too deep. So deep that it hurts, and the only way to soothe the ache is to close my eyes and surrender.

My traitorous body was made for him. The way he feels is almost too much for my brain to process all at once. Massive. Unending. *Gentle.*

I marvel at that fact more than any other. He braces his hand beneath me to keep my back from contacting the rough wood of the headboard, even though the act forces him into an awkward crouch. It's almost like he doesn't even realize he's doing it—shouldering the discomfort entirely on his own.

He's too busy tasting any part of me his tongue can reach. My shoulder. My throat. Soon, meaningless words meld with every wet flick of heat. "So beautiful...beautiful. So fucking good."

Sergei is a distant memory as long as I stay here in Mischa's arms, treasured and hated at the same damn time. My heart hammers into a frantic melody, matching the pace of his as our breathing slows and our sweat dries.

Eventually, he tries to pull back, but my limbs stiffen, keeping him captive for once. *My* prisoner. Unlike his increasing demands, I only want one thing from him.

Oblivion.

And for whatever reason…

He stays here, giving me a taste.

CHAPTER 3

"*D*id you really think you could fool me?"

I startle awake and find a shadow looming over me. With rough hands, it rips the blankets from my body, leaving me naked in the frigid air.

"So, *this* is your game," the specter growls, brandishing something in his fist.

A photograph? Whoever took it must have been only able to capture their subject from afar. In the dark, I can barely make out anything of substance.

Anything other than a small figure sporting a mop of brilliant blond hair.

My brain shuts down, refusing to connect the dots. It's like I'm sleepwalking, processing everything two seconds too slow. Mischa's anger. The unfamiliar boy in the photo. The torn remnants of an envelope sprinkled over the floor…

"No!" Reality slams into me all at once, and I lunge from the bed, snatching at the picture. "No!"

"Oh, *yes*." Laughing, Mischa steps back, dangling the photo beyond my reach. "Are you really that fucking stupid? What did Sergei promise you? A happily fucking ever after with your precious Robert and his goddamn spawn—"

"Stop! Stop! Stop!" I lash out with my nails drawn, striking any part of him I can reach. His skin is iron, reinforced by steel muscles, and each blow hurts me more than him. Regardless, I slap and punch and bite.

It's all I can do.

"Stop it!" Abruptly, he retaliates, grabbing my wrists. "Enough!" I can barely hear him above the rush of blood surging through my ears. "I said enough!"

"Why would you do this?" I've been shouting at him all this time. The same broken words, over and over. "Why? Why?"

My knees buckle, and he lunges, looping his arm around my waist. Even as I struggle, he remains the only force keeping me upright.

"Stop," he growls.

"Why?" His chest is the only refuge. My tears sink into the cotton of his shirt as I wrestle one of my hands from his grip and slam it harmlessly against him. "Why? I let it go... I didn't listen. I *can't* listen. Why? Why?"

"I'm sorry."

"Why? Why? Why—"

"I'm *sorry*! Do you fucking hear me?" He shakes me so violently that my head rears back and forth against my shoulders. When I go limp, he grits his teeth and something in his expression gives way. Guilt? "I'm sorry, all right?"

"Rip it up," I demand, squeezing my eyes shut. "Do it now. Rip it up!"

"Fuck… Okay!" He sighs.

But I can't breathe until I hear the telltale hiss of paper tearing. Suddenly, all the tension leaves my body, which sends me crashing to my knees.

"Hey!"

Fire engulfs me from above. I'm in his arms again, held stiffly as if he half expects me to continue attacking him. But all I can do is grip his shoulders, sinking my nails in.

"Don't ever mention him—never," I rasp. "Never. Never—"

"I won't." His voice drips into my ear, callously mocking. "I'll just talk about *you*."

Stung, I try to twist from his reach, but his arms tighten like a bear trap, crushing me to his chest.

"I'll talk about how good you feel when you drop the nun act." His mouth slips into the space between my shoulder and my throat, nuzzling the tender flesh there. "So good. Too good. I never taught you how to bite."

Against my will, my limbs relax, which leaves me at his mercy. In response, his fingers catch at my hair, sinking through the tangled strands, surprisingly gentle.

"And that mouth. I will teach you how to use that properly." His voice deepens to a merciless hum. "I'll have you on your knees every fucking day, Rose. But you're so damn selfish. I'll have to use mine first, won't I?"

He pauses but doesn't seem to expect an answer.

"I'm going to make you beg for it though," he muses, running his fingers along my scalp. "I'll make you beg… And we have all the time in the goddamn world. I intend to make use of every fucking second."

His threats shouldn't feel like a welcome reprieve. His grated, malicious tone shouldn't be enough to drive Sergei and his ultimatum away.

Violent lust shouldn't be a comfort.

But it is.

I wake up alone, splayed out on the floor with a musty pillow shoved beneath my head and a threadbare blanket draped over me. Chaos resonates from the hall, presumably what drew me awake. An attack?

My ears strain in an attempt to decipher the stomping footsteps and raised voices.

"Who said you could get out of bed?" Mischa's voice reaches me from beyond the door—but I'm not his victim for once. And he sounds different now from the harsh growl I'm used to. Almost…playful?

"Fine," he snaps. "You think you can handle it? Go get dressed."

Curious, I climb to my feet, bracing myself against the bedframe for balance. My dress is a crumpled heap tossed in a corner. Creeping toward it, I drag it on and advance to the door. Before I can reach for the knob, it's opened from the outside.

The intruder grunts, startled by the sight of me standing here.

He's changed into a fresh set of fatigues. In the shadows of the hall, his eyes gleam, flicking over me in a callous swipe. My chest constricts as I brace for an insult. Or maybe a cruel reminder of the night before?

Instead, he inclines his head and then advances down the hall, leaving me to follow. Seconds pass as I contemplate whether or not I should.

Playing with him is a dangerous game of hide-and-seek. My soul is the prize, and he's ruthless in his pursuit. Just when I think I've found a safe place, he pounces from the shadows, eager to rip me to shreds.

"Are you coming?" he wonders from the bottom of the stairs.

Only when someone whizzes past do I realize he wasn't speaking to me.

Mouse skips toward him, her hair in disarray. Wearing an oversized gray shirt as a makeshift dress, she looks younger than ever. The only clue of her injury is a slight stiffness in her left shoulder as she bounds down the stairs.

"Let's play a game," Mischa proposes when she appears at his side. His voice is louder than it needs to be. For my benefit, I suspect. He relishes in the fact that I'm spying. "How not to get shot or killed if we're attacked. You have five seconds to run and hide." He cocks his head and makes a shooing motion with his hand. "One… Two…"

Mouse takes off through the front door, navigating awkwardly over the uneven terrain beyond it.

"Don't go beyond the clearing," Mischa warns.

But three seconds later, he still hasn't followed after her.

Only when I'm halfway down the staircase does he finally jolt into motion and stroll into the pale dawn. God knows why I follow him.

It's cold out and my thin, filthy dress is no match. Mouse must be freezing as well, though Mischa doesn't seem bothered by the chill. His shoulders are set with determination—he's a man on a mission, apparently.

Paces away from him, I can no longer stay silent. "This is a cruel idea of a game."

"Can you think of a better way for her to learn?" he counters. "Or should she just cower in a corner the next time your husband's men come knocking?"

He looks over his shoulder, revealing the anger smoldering in his gaze. Maybe a hint of blame lurks there as well. I caused this.

Swallowing hard, I turn away from him and find myself eyeing the wooded clearing surrounding the safe house. The stone cottage might have been a family home once. A secluded haven possessing a flower patch, a small yard, and a rickety shed.

But now? It's a makeshift fort in a two-man war.

"Is it even safe to be out here?" I ask. "I don't see your men."

The trees looming a short distance from the house provide only minimal protection. There's no gate. No barbed wire. Nothing to slow a bullet or a trained soldier. I jump as underbrush crunches nearby and my heart hammers, spurring my unease. In every swaying shadow, I see danger. Movement. Robert.

"It's safe enough," Mischa boasts, suddenly closer. "And my men know how to hide, Rose. So don't get any cute ideas of running."

I hunch away from him, hugging my arms around my torso. "What is this place anyway?"

"Property," he snaps. "And, for now, any Winthorp spies should steer clear. Your good friend Sergei has ensured that.

Either way." He shrugs, scanning the area surrounding the clearing. "She needs to learn."

I bristle at the seriousness in his tone. "Learn what?"

"How the Winthorps play: dirty." He fixates on a distant part of the yard where, at first glance, I see nothing.

Then a glimmer of golden hair flashes between a thicket of branches.

"Bang!" Mischa bellows, letting his voice ring throughout the clearing. Startled birds scatter in every which direction, and I marvel at his confidence. Despite his mistrust of the older Vasilev, he truly doesn't seem worried. "I've found you. Try again."

A dejected Mouse limps from around the base of a tree, her lips pursed. My pity lasts only seconds before she disappears again.

But not for long.

"Pathetic," Mischa snarls a minute later. His new target is a monstrous pile of chopped wood. "You can't hesitate. Try again."

Sure enough, Mouse darts into sight and then races away.

For what feels like hours, he makes her hide before discovering her easily. Over and over. Behind brambles. Or trees, or sections of the house.

Finally, he advances toward another tree, huffing in exasperation.

"You're dead," he declares, yanking her from her hiding place. "You need to be more careful—"

"Mischa…" I watch my hand brush over his shoulder before I even register touching him.

"What?" He glares at my fingers and then follows my gaze toward Mouse.

She stands awkwardly in his grasp, huddled against the bark of the tree. In the pale light, it's easy to make out a silvery substance glinting on her cheeks. Tears.

I start toward her, but Mischa crouches on one knee and grabs her arm, turning her to face him.

"I've scared you, haven't I?"

The shift in his tone stops me in my tracks. The gruff soldier I know is replaced by…a man. One who sounds repentant.

"I'm sorry." He reaches out to smooth a stray piece of hair behind her ear. "But I don't want you to get hurt again. Do you understand?"

Swiping at her streaming eyes, Mouse nods. Her face is red, her mouth trembling. But her brave veneer is no match when Mischa coaxes her into his arms and stands, lifting her entirely.

"I *can't* see you hurt again," he repeats, his voice low, just for her. "So if I have to teach you to hide so that no one can ever get close enough, I will…"

His gaze turns distant, and I don't think he realizes what he's doing: holding the girl in his arms so tight that no one could ever rip her away. He isn't here but years in the past. With his sister, Aljona?

"I know." My heart pounds as I step forward, though I'm not sure why I intervene at all. "Let's play another game."

They both jump at the sound of my voice. Aware of their scrutiny, I stoop and pluck a wildflower from an unruly patch at my feet. Pale blue, its thin petals stand out in stark contrast against the gray, overcast sky above.

"This is the most valuable thing in the world," I say, holding it out to Mouse.

Still trapped in Mischa's embrace, she eyes it warily before finally clasping her fingers around the stalk.

"You need to protect it," I tell her. "Protect it with everything you have. And him?" I point to Mischa. "He's the monster you're guarding it from."

Mischa meets my gaze, his look long and searching. Finally, he releases Mouse and sighs. "You heard her. Go!"

The girl takes off, slipping between the trees.

In her wake, the silence is so oppressive, like a noose around my throat. I can't take it.

So like any prisoner sentenced to death, I meet my end with little fanfare.

"I forgive you," I say thickly.

Seemingly intent on his prey, Mischa doesn't even acknowledge I've spoken. But he's listening. His shoulders tense with every word.

"And you can sneer and shrug it off. But I do. I refuse to let my life be ruled by petty grudges—"

"Forgiveness." He grunts as if the concept is too foreign to understand. But, to my shock, when I glance at his face, I don't find a smirk. He merely sighs, running his fingers through his wild hair. "As you say, Rose."

"And I want you to know something." The wind carries my voice to him. I'm too tired to put any effort into the sound myself. I merely mouth the words and hope they escape the prison of my throat. "Something I've never told anyone else…" I tilt my head toward the breeze, letting it lick away the dried tears clinging to my skin.

Above, the sky looms a stormy gray. The swirling clouds could be trying to warn me, growing darker by the second. Or maybe the building tempest is just goading me on. *You've been broken already. What could be worse?*

"I don't know what love is," I admit. Out loud, it sounds so simple. So pathetic. "I don't know if I've ever loved Robert. I don't think I've ever loved anyone—not really. Not even my mother… I don't know what it feels like to worry for someone so much you can't bear to see them hurt. I don't know what it's like to…" I trail off. After licking my lips, I try again, but the words stick in my throat, so stupid. So raw. So desperate. I have to force them out. "I can't even mourn my own sister the way you can—"

"Are you calling me emotional, Little Rose?" He cuts his gaze in my direction.

"No. But…I'm jealous of you." I turn away from him as my cheeks catch flame. What am I even saying? "I don't know," I say. "I wish I knew what it was like…"

To be so rabid with affection, even as you rip apart anyone stupid enough to desire to get close.

"What it's like?" he asks.

I flinch as his hand latches onto the back of my scalp and steers me forward. Without warning, he presses me against the bark of a tree, stopping just short of grinding my face against it.

"So that you can manipulate me, Little Rose?" he pants against my shoulder. "Continue to spin your little web?"

I go limp, laughing softly to myself. Of course the bastard can't let his guard down for a second. Even in the rare instance when I try to lower mine.

"So that I can understand you," I gasp out to an ant crawling, inches from my cheek. It jolts and changes direction, scurrying away. "All I want is to understand you."

It's the only way I will ever beat him at his own game.

"Love?" Mischa echoes. He steps into me, fanning his hands out over my waist. "I'll tell you a little secret: It's pain, Rose. It's wanting someone so fucking much—but you don't know why. It's feeling them crawl beneath your goddamn skin. They're in your head. In your skull. Laughing at you.

Taunting you. You want to love?" He laughs and each unsteady cackle sears the flesh of my jaw. "I could fucking drown you in it—"

Nearby, a branch cracks, presumably snapped underfoot, and Mischa pulls away.

"I can hear you," he calls out to the creeping figure. Grabbing my wrist, he tugs me along as he picks his way between the trees. "Slow down," he warns, stopping short. He cocks his head, letting his ear pick up the slightest noise. "That's it. Get your bearings. I still haven't spotted you. Use this to your advantage. Don't panic. *Think*."

I strain my eyes, hunting for any hint of what he's sensing. The seconds trickle by painfully slow, but I don't catch a glimpse of her. Apparently, neither does Mischa.

"Good!" His laugh booms out proudly, a mark of approval. "*Very* good." He resumes his prowling stance and inches forward. "Now, let's see how long you can keep it up…"

CHAPTER 4

We hunt for her long after the early morning stretches into the afternoon. If Mischa has more pressing business to attend to, he doesn't let on. So intent on his lesson, he doesn't seem to notice the passage of time.

Finally, he places his hand on my shoulder, motioning for me to stay back. Alone, he stalks to a nearby tree, barely making a sound over the brambles.

"There you are!" He lunges forward and reaches around the trunk. "Found you—"

His snatching fingers come up empty, however. He frowns at them, his eyebrows furrowing. Then, almost in comically slow motion, an acorn falls from a higher branch, hitting him squarely in the middle of his forehead.

He jerks back, looking up.

And at that exact moment, a grinning Mouse unfurls herself from a twisted thicket of branches.

Mischa's expression ripples, eerily stern. Then he laughs and claps his hands. "Good! Very good." Still clapping, he watches her climb down and then ruffles her hair. "Much better."

Mouse grins. Very carefully, she opens one of her fists, revealing the flower tucked against her palm. If she were one to gloat, I can imagine what she might say. *I win.*

"Show-off." Mischa's upper lip twitches, resisting the smile that transforms his mouth regardless. "Now, come. We should get back before Ivan starts grumbling."

Skipping ahead, Mouse leads the way through the trees, back to the house.

As predicted, Vanya greets us near the front door, his lips pursed. How long has he been watching us from afar? I can't tell.

Neither can I decipher if he recalls our conversation from last night. His gaze flits over me before settling on the figure prancing nearby.

"You're a mess," he grumbles to Mouse, beckoning her inside. "Come on. I'll get you something to eat, and then it's back to bed." To Mischa, he inclines his head respectfully. "The perimeter is still secure according to the men. Sergei wasn't lying. But..." He cuts his gaze in my direction. Then he shrugs, deeming me worthy to hear his concerns. "I don't like it. I say we move as soon as possible. It will be risky, but—"

"When haven't I been up for a risk?" Mischa finishes for him. "Make the preparations. We can move out in the morning."

"As you wish." Nodding, Vanya reenters the house.

I start to follow, but Misha grabs my wrist before I can slip past him.

"Wait. It's time for another game," he says, his voice grated. "I'm not in the mood for flower picking, so consider *yourself* the prize." He shoves me toward a section of forest. "So run."

I stagger forward, maneuvering as quickly as I can over the uneven terrain. There's no way I can outrun him. As my knees buckle, I haul myself behind the nearest tree and wait. Anticipation wracks my spine, heightening the hiss of every swaying branch and rustling leaf.

"Child's play," Mischa hisses, advancing at a lazy pace. He doesn't even try to hide the sound of his footsteps, which crunch sticks and undergrowth with every step. "If you make it this easy, then what is the fucking point?"

A million familiar sensations curdle in my stomach. *Caught. Trapped. Helpless. Hopeless.* Sighing, I lean against the bark, impatient for the inevitable.

Almost as if my hiding place is mocking my cowardice, something falls from a branch and lands at my feet. Small.

Round. An acorn. My eyes fixate on its brown surface as Mischa's advice to Mouse replays in my head: *Don't panic. Think.*

I can't outsmart him for long—but he's a wolf. Predators like him don't expect their prey to fight back.

"Found you," he hisses paces from my hiding spot. So smug in his capture, he doesn't attempt to hide his attack; a shadow rushing toward me warns the second he reaches out.

So I pivot in the opposite direction.

"Where are you—" His back is to me now.

I'm the wolf, and my attack comes swiftly: I lunge. Before I can reach him, he twists around with feline grace. But he's too late. Grunting, he's forced to catch me by the waist, but he can't defend from the palm I press against the center of his chest.

"Bang," I tell him coldly, meeting his widening gaze. "You're dead."

I expect him to shove me off. Or, better yet, leave me here in an exhausted heap. I'm so tired of fighting him at every turn.

But rather than let me go, he grips me tighter, moving his face near mine until they touch. Cheek to cheek. We share the same twisted breath.

"*This* is why you are more dangerous than the Winthorps and their army combined," he murmurs, digging his fingers into my hips for emphasis. "You are reckless. Nothing is sacred to you. You'll burn your enemies and yourself down in the same fucking blaze. Even the most sick, twisted bastards aren't that cruel."

An amusing thought comes to me, and I voice it near his ear. "Does that scare you?"

A harsh grunt catches in his throat. He sets me down but then captures my chin, forcing me to look up. His gaze bores through mine with a predatory accuracy. From this assault, there is no escape.

And I know now that his "game" has nothing at all to do with hide-and-seek.

"Look at me." His irises darken, a piercing, unsettling shade of black. "Tell me... Tell me how it feels when I'm inside you."

"W-what?" My cheeks catch fire at the crude request. Another sick joke? But no. His eyes are too open, meeting my probing stare unflinchingly.

"You heard me." He wants an answer, and my throat rasps as I try to compile one.

"It feels like sex—"

"No." His thumb swipes at my lower lip, dismissing the response. "Don't play coy. You were upset last night—but you came to *me*. I want to know why."

His expression shifts, and I catch a glimpse of the stranger I've only ever seen with Mouse. The exhausted man with shadows beneath his eyes. Worn lines distort the skin around his mouth, and his voice is so much clearer than the rough grumble I'm used to. Panicked, I realize it's his most lethal weapon, this guttural hum.

"Tell me—"

"Too much." I close my eyes against his judgment, but I can't seem to make myself stop talking. "You feel too big. Like all you want to do is rip me open, and there is nothing I can do to stop it. I…I don't want to stop it…" I sway as his grip loosens. But bit by bit, it tightens again, drawing me closer.

"Why?" he demands. "Tell me."

"When you kiss me… I can't think. And I don't want to."

I doubt he understands just how dangerous an admission that is. In my entire life, my only saving grace was my ability to think. Override my body's natural instincts. Endure.

Until now.

"It feels real," I whisper, horrified. "I can't ignore it. I can't suppress it. What you do to me feels so damn real—"

Moist heat rips my voice from me. His mouth—I've memorized the shape. It conforms to mine like nothing else, designed to overpower and subdue. Claim. One teasing brush of his tongue and my thoughts empty of anything tangible. All I can do is cling to him, pawing at his shoulders for purchase.

I'm vaguely aware that he's moving, backing me against the very same tree I attacked him from. Viciously, his hands sink into my hair, gripping tight as he draws back, breaking the kiss.

"I'll give it to him," he says, laughing in a broken, hollow series of grunts. "If you really are a skilled fucking spy—a trick… Then I have to hand it to him. I give in." His eyes meet mine again, unfocused and crazed. Truly insane. "You've fucking done it. He's won. I'm a pathetic fucking idiot. So here—" He grinds his pelvis into mine. "Savor your victory, Rose."

Savor. I run my hands down his chest, the planes of it rippling beneath the thin layer of cotton. In the darkness, I can't see the skin bared beneath as he wrenches it up over his head and tosses it aside. I have to feel every inch for myself.

Raw. Powerful. Broken and healed in some places, still wounded and sore in others. He lets me have my fill of tracing every inch of his armor. I barely even notice when his hands slip beneath my dress, ruthlessly turning the tables.

"You're so damn wet." He hisses that assessment even before his fingers dip between my legs, finding his boast to be true. "You *have* to be a fucking trick," he declares, breaching me with the pad of his thumb. "There's no other way…"

He doesn't elaborate. Once again, our conversation devolves into the unspoken. Grasping touches that convey more than words ever could. Slow, rasping breaths when he yanks his pants down and eases his way inside me.

My eyes flutter shut at the sensation.

"Tell me now," he snarls into my neck. "Tell me."

"You feel…"

He slows, panting against my throat. "Say it." Impatient, he thrusts again, utilizing his body like a battering ram.

I'm no match for him. "You feel so good," I whimper. "So, so good."

He groans, forging a frantic rhythm within seconds. Savor my victory, he told me, but there's no time. No chance. He overdoses me on his touch, taste—everything all at once.

"Beautiful Little Rose," he taunts as I shatter. "You win. You win. But I'll play your game: I'll drag you down with me. I'll destroy you—we'll both go up in flames."

And he breaks me, leaving me in pieces against the rough, unyielding bark.

But in the aftermath of him, I've never felt clearer.

And I've never felt more powerful.

We redress in silence and return to the house just as the moon rises to its highest point in the sky. Vanya still waits by the front door, watchfully eyeing the dark. As we slip inside, he casts us both a searching glance.

Once again, his gaze skims over me and settles on someone else.

"Mischa." He places his hand on the younger man's shoulder. "We need to talk—"

"If this is about leaving, I agree," Mischa says, shoving me through the doorway ahead of him. "We move out early. I'll take the lead. You pick up the rear and then we'll regroup—"

"That's not what I mean." Vanya sighs and I catch his gaze dart down the hall leading deeper into the house. "There is something—"

"What?" Mischa strokes his chin. "Are you worried about Sergei? Maybe we shouldn't inform the old man just yet. Not until we have a clear route."

"I have a suggestion." That voice…

My shock matches Mischa's as none other than Sergei appears at the mouth of the hall.

"Speak of the devil," Mischa growls under his breath. His grip on my arm tightens and I can feel the tension radiating off him in waves.

"Sorry to intrude," the older man says, though his expression reveals no ounce of guilt. He approaches us at a cautious pace, dressed head to toe in a practical black outfit that sets him apart from Mischa's filthy fatigues. "But I think it will be more prudent if a group of my men leads the way. Then you can follow. With Winthorp on the prowl, you should center your retreat around his biggest target."

"Oh?" Mischa raises an eyebrow. "And what would that be?"

"*Who*," Sergei corrects, turning to me. "Her."

"And let me guess. That biggest threat will stay with you?"

"No." Sergei shakes his head, raising his hands in a subtle sign of surrender. "I'll go with my men."

The two men eye each other, tension crackling between them.

"It's a good plan, Mischa," Vanya pipes up. He moves, positioning himself between his brother and his surrogate son. "I say we use his method and move out tomorrow night. That will give us time to plan a safe route."

"Fine." Eyes flashing, Mischa flexes his arm, dragging me closer to his side. "But she will stay with *me* and *you* will lead the way."

"Fair enough." Sergei nods. "As Ivan suggested, we can move tomorrow night, before the sun rises."

"Fine." Mischa releases me and barges deeper into the house, barking out orders.

Seemingly from nowhere, his men converge on the narrow space, pushing the limits of the cottage to their max. Once Mischa's plan is relayed in detail, they disperse to carry out their given orders and I can feel their leader's eyes on me as I make my way to the stairs.

"Wait."

I stiffen with one foot braced on the lower step. He takes his time coming up behind me. His finger teasingly ghosts my cheek before his entire hand pulls a lock of hair back from my face.

"Look at me."

He's frowning when I do, scanning my gaze. For what? I'm not sure. Only that the hunt for it hollows his features, and the line of his mouth is tighter as he turns away.

"Go run up to bed, Little Rose," he commands. "Maybe if you pray hard enough, the monsters will stay out of it tonight."

I obey, racing up the stairs. Once inside my small room, I find myself paralyzed by the sight of the rumpled bed, its blankets strewn all over the floor.

In the end, I brace my back against the wall and sink down to my knees, forsaking the comfort of the mattress.

The cold floor, with its covering of dust, is more welcome than any ounce of softness containing his scent.

Even if it means I suffer.

A groan escapes my lips as I open my eyes to the dim glow of dawn filtering in through the room's only window. Already, I thoroughly regret my decision to forsake the bed. My legs throb when I attempt to stand, and I have to ease myself upright, using the wall like a makeshift ladder.

Sighing, I eye my filthy clothing and make a halfhearted trip around the room in search of anything else to wear.

So much for the new Ellen. Gone are my handpicked clothes, lost in the flames that consumed Mischa's manor.

Unsurprisingly, I find nothing here, which leaves only one other course of action to feel somewhat cleaner.

I steel myself as I approach the door and palm the knob. When I finally gather the nerve to push it open, I don't find any madmen lurking beyond it.

But I do discover a bathroom not far from my hideaway. It's small but contains a tub at least. Despite a circle of rust around the drain, the plumbing seems to be in working order.

After stripping my clothing, I climb inside and run the water as hot as I can stand it. Then I huddle in the center of the basin and struggle to find some semblance of peace. It's surprisingly easy. As the heat sinks into my limbs and licks away the grime on my skin, I rest my head against the rim of the tub and close my eyes.

A sudden thud cuts my reprieve short. The door opens, slamming against the wall, and the source of my unease enters.

I lurch upright, shielding my breasts with trembling hands. "What are you doing?"

Mischa scoffs, eyeing my body as boldly as if he owns every inch. "Don't tell me a haughty woman of your esteem plans to wear the same dirty clothing." He extends his hand, revealing a wad of material I didn't notice before. Fabric? He unfolds it for my inspection: a thick, gray shirt like the kind Mouse wore the other day.

But I doubt it will fit me as well as it fit her.

"Don't stick your nose up just yet," Mischa warns. Up until now, he was obscuring another garment behind his back: a pair of black pants. "I took these from the smallest man in my crew, but I doubt they'll fit you well enough. You'll just have to make do."

He tosses both garments onto the floor near the tub.

"Thank you," I croak, surprised despite myself. It's like he read my mind. Though maybe he can? He scans my features as easily as one would an open book.

"Thank me? For ensuring that you *don't* get the idea to walk around naked and tempt my men into doing your bidding?"

I scoff and turn my attention to my limbs. Steam rises from the basin of the tub as my legs redden in the heat.

"Doesn't it exhaust you?" I wonder. "Being so damn paranoid?"

A sound escapes his throat, but I can't decipher it. A laugh?

"Paranoid? I call it prudent." He turns from me and lifts his shirt over his head, tossing it to his feet.

My eyes scan his body appreciatively before I can help it. His tattoos gleam, melding with his healing scrapes and wounds. The man is a canvas of darkness and blood. If I believed in demons, I'd wholeheartedly insist he was one. Sin in the flesh.

"See something you like?" he wonders.

Licking my lips, I croak, "What are you doing?"

"Are you the only one allowed to be clean?" He braces his hands over the rusty sink and leans in toward the mirror, observing his reflection. Whatever he finds makes him turn away and fish a rag from beneath the sink. After sniffing it, he shrugs. Apparently, it's clean enough.

He wets it beneath the faucet and swipes at his face.

Watching him, I find that the only way to regain my composure is by utilizing the one weapon proven effective against him.

Speaking.

"You seem pretty calm," I remark as I stretch out my sore legs. "For a man whose home just burned to the ground."

He stiffens, and in the mirror, I catch his fleeting scowl.

"I've had many homes," he says simply. Setting the rag aside, he wets his fingers and rakes them through his tangled hair. "Unlike you and your Winthorps, I don't get attached to a pretty dwelling."

"But that place was different," I point out. "You called it by a name once. Pecavi?"

He ignores me, still combing through his hair.

But I can't fathom his indifference. "Your mother's things. Your sister's... Won't you miss them?"

He pushes back from the sink, but when he faces me, he doesn't look angry. "And do you miss *your* mother's things?" He eyes my neck.

I reach up automatically, clasping the tiny charm dangling against my collar.

"Don't," he scolds, and a curious thought makes me loosen my grip over my necklace. Have I insulted him? It seems I have. He's still frowning. "I've had plenty of chances to take it from you—"

"I never had anything of hers to hold on to before," I admit, referring to his previous question. "Not even a button or ring."

"Well, I'd give up a million *things*." He stoops for his shirt and pulls it on over his head. "Everything, to have more than a memory. And to avenge them, I will endure many fires and occupy a million fucking houses. Nothing ever changes."

It's a cold outlook. And a lonely one.

"So you don't cherish anything?" I ask.

"What's the point?" He shrugs and then jerks his chin to the running faucet of the tub. "Don't spend the day wasting away, Little Rose." He approaches the door and opens it, heedless of who might be walking by on the other end. "You need to be ready to move. Tonight."

"To another safe house?"

"You better hope so." He steps over the threshold, closing the door behind him. Regardless, his voice reaches me through the wood. "Because the only alternative is a

Winthorp prison. At least with me, your fashion choices differ from a ball and chain."

I listen to his steps retreat and hug myself as the water cools. By the time I finally climb out of the tub, I'm shivering. Thankfully, Mischa's clothing provides a decent amount of warmth, and the pants aren't uncomfortable. If I roll the hems a few times, they almost fit.

When I reenter the hall fully dressed, I can hear Mischa down below, marshaling his men to various tasks.

He claimed that property meant nothing to him, but I think it was a lie.

He's comfortable like this, living in transience. There's no stability to rely upon and nothing he could risk losing other than his life.

And if Mischa Stepanov seems to value one thing least of all.

It's himself.

CHAPTER 6

I spend the day lurking in the shadows of the property with no real purpose other than to bide my time. For lunch, I eat with Mouse, who barely acknowledges my presence.

While she may communicate with Mischa easily, any question I voice her way goes ignored.

Alone, I settle into the corners of the house, watching Mischa from afar.

Did he mean the words he groaned to me in the forest?

Or perhaps his more recent boast conveys his true feelings? *Nothing is worth holding on to for long.*

Though the man does seem to cherish his power. He wields it effortlessly, almost without realizing the control he has over people.

"Get ready," he says to me, noticing my silent observation once night has fallen. "Sergei will be here soon. His roaches are already scurrying around." He nods to a man standing silently among the quiet chaos of packing and coordination going on around him. Instead of fatigues, he's wearing black from head to toe and his build is sturdier than the agile men in Mischa's crew. "Keep an eye on him and his little friends," Mischa warns as I spot several other darkly dressed figures stationed at various points in the safe house.

"Spy on them?" I ask, but I'm intrigued despite myself. "Aren't they on your side?"

"Side." He scoffs, turning away. "Just tell me if they look too jumpy."

I'm bored enough to take him up on his offer.

Unfortunately, Sergei's men make for boring targets to spy on. They barely move even a step out of place. With a focused intensity, they observe Mischa's men as disinterestedly as I observe them.

Eventually, it becomes obvious that the scruffy outlaw leader is a much more interesting target.

I find myself creeping into the hallway just to keep watch as he directs the movement of vans in the yard and dishes out more orders. The shadows of the house paint him, highlighting the contrast of gold and darkness that make up his core.

Strip him of the scars and tattoos and he could have been a different man in another life. Someone honorable. A teacher sternly directing students? Or a police officer? It's terrifying how many possibilities could fit someone like him, armed with both authority and charm.

Redefining him consumes my focus—and I don't even notice someone beside me until it's too late. They brush past me and I jump, jarring my shoulder off the wall.

"Excuse me, miss," the figure says, placing a steadying grip on my forearm. "Are you all right?"

"I'm fine," I rasp automatically. Even so, my fingers rub at the back of my neck as I look up into the stern features of one of Sergei's "roaches."

"My apologies," he murmurs. "Let me make sure I didn't—"

"You can let her go," Mischa quietly insists from the entrance to the cottage. His eyes fixate on the man's hand until he releases me, and I smother a sigh. It's like he's hardwired to sense the moment any other dog might so much as sniff the air near his coveted prize. "Besides." He glances over his shoulder, frowning. "Your master is here."

Sergei enters the cottage a heartbeat later. He and Mischa lock gazes, trading a million warnings between them, I suspect. Together, they move into the sitting room off the hall. Someone left a paper map unfurled over the couch and Sergei points to it, stroking his chin with his opposite hand.

"Did you have a destination in mind?" he asks.

"West." Mischa positions himself near the doorway, his arms crossed. When I creep up beside him, he looks at me but says nothing. Returning his attention to Sergei, he adds, "I have a cabin there."

"Another safe house?" Sergei raises an eyebrow. "May I make a suggestion?"

Mischa grunts. "I doubt I can refuse."

"I suggest we regroup at my property. It's close. It's familiar, and I can supply more comfort to your guests than some shack in the woods."

"Fine," Mischa grates through clenched teeth. "We can go now. Gather your men. Lead the way."

"As you wish." Sergei exits the house, but paces down the front path, he calls back, "There is one thing we need to discuss, however…"

"Oh?" Mischa's eyes narrow, eternally suspicious, and I'm close enough to catch that. "And what is that?"

"Where is Ivan?"

Mischa purses his lips. "I had him scout ahead," he finally admits. "Why?"

"Because," Sergei calls, sounding farther from the cottage. "We need to discuss what he might do when I tell him about his daughter."

"Have you gone insane—" Mischa breaks off, glancing at me. "Don't move," he snarls before marching out to meet Sergei.

He shouts something. That's all I'm aware of as I approach the doorway in their wake, despite Mischa's warning. For some reason, I'm still swiping at my neck…but something's wrong.

My limbs feel heavy.

Too heavy.

My hand goes limp, falling to my side, and I sway, forced to lean against the wall for balance.

I can still hear Mischa growling something to Sergei paces away.

"Mi…" I try to speak. Cry out. Anything.

But with every attempt, I make less noise.

Until the world goes silent entirely, and I fall into a sea of black.

I come to on a firm surface. The floor? No… The plush material beneath me isn't the harsh wood of the safe house. Have we moved already? My head throbs as I try to remember.

Mischa…

Sergei...

They were talking about Vanya—but anything after is an ominous blank. One fact I am aware of, however, is that the figure standing over me, reeking of cologne, is not Mischa.

My eyes fly open and I look up, scrambling into a crouch. Sluggish limbs rob me of any grace, and I have to brace both of my hands against the unfamiliar carpet beneath me to stay upright.

"You've been drugged, miss," the man says matter-of-factly. His face is strange. He isn't wearing the gray fatigues of Mischa or his men, either. In stark contrast, a crisp black suit differentiates him entirely. "The effects should wear off in a few minutes," he continues. "But to minimize any risk to yourself, I suggest you relax."

"Sergei," I rasp while blinking to bring the rest of our surroundings into clearer focus. We're in a room with one exit—and the man just so happens to be positioned closer to it: a door opened only to shadow.

The room itself is spacious, containing a lavish bed draped in red sheets and a wooden wardrobe. Rich burgundy wallpaper betrays a finery I've only seen matched in Mischa's manor as of yet. Is this place the property Sergei mentioned? My throat aches as I cling to that possibility—it has to be.

"Do you work for him?" I ask the man. "Sergei—"

"No." The reply comes from someone else who appears in the doorway like a phantom in a nightmare.

Chilling familiarity paralyzes me, snuffing any ounce of air from my lungs. As I suffocate, I dig my nails into my palms, hoping the pain jars me awake.

I'm dreaming.

I have to be…

"He works for me," the newcomer says, his voice a suave, polished tenor. "And he finally fucking earned his keep. Elle."

Dressed in black, my husband surges forward. He cut his hair in my absence, though it's styled in its familiar elegant coif. He's as tall as I remember, but his thin build casts less intimidation than Mischa's bulk. It's his bruised, swollen left hand that draws my attention the most.

And it's his eyes that make my heart hammer unsteadily.

Amber like fire, they brim with rage.

"You're safe," he swears, sinking to one knee. He reaches for me only to stop short inches from my face.

Because I'm filthy, reeking of dust, and the forest, and Mischa Stepanov.

CHAPTER 7

This nightmare doesn't end when Robert pulls away and stands. I'm painfully awake and aware of every ounce of freedom slipping through my grasping fingers.

This isn't a nightmare…

This is hell.

"She needs a bath," Robert declares, gesturing to my body. "And send for the doctor immediately."

"Yes, sir." As if conjured from nothing, a woman appears by his side. Her plain dress denotes her as a maid, and she obediently stoops beside me, helping me to my feet.

"And rest," Robert adds. His eyes sweep me over, brimming with rage I've never seen his aristocratic features manifest before. Hatred. Loathing. Fear? "I'll make them pay," he swears. "Those bastards will fucking pay."

Have they already been captured? I try to picture Mischa and Vanya in chains as my gaze returns to Robert's bruised hand. He holds it awkwardly, but judging from the greenish hue of his skin, I doubt it's a fresh injury.

Despite everything, I can't stay silent.

"Is he alive?" I force myself to ask. "Mis—"

"Stepanov?" Robert frowns and a familiar unease gathers in my stomach.

In so many ways, he's the same man I was taken from. But there's an aged quality to his gaze that wasn't there before. A darkness. Gone is his old childhood ring Mischa presented to me on a bloody platter as well. In its place gleams a new, more prominent piece of jewelry: the heavier insignia I've seen worn only by his father.

"I'll kill him," he swears, brushing the tip of his finger along my cheek—as much of himself as he can bear to taint. "I'll rip him to pieces. He will pay."

But he hasn't. Not yet. A painful emotion flutters in my chest as I sway, relying on the maid for support. I can't even find a name for it until Robert finally leaves the room, flanked by his henchman.

Maybe it's terror.

Or perhaps…

It's hope.

*T*he maid bathes me without uttering a single word—but where Mouse's silence seemed stubborn at times, hers is deliberate.

There are no mocking taunts as she strips my clothing and coaxes me into the steaming tub of an ornate bathroom. There is no softness to her touch as she drags a rag over my bruised, swollen limbs. All in all, I'm treated mechanically, like a broken, battered object in need of restoration.

She doesn't even look me in the eye as she washes my hair and combs through the ragged strands. To her, I am merely a doll dressed in a gossamer nightgown and led back into the room I woke up in like a lamb to slaughter.

My breath catches at the sight of the bed. It's large enough for two people—and only one fact makes it possible to breathe again. Some things never change, and Robert Winthorp is a creature I've studied cover to cover.

As Mischa claimed, he never shared my bed. And he won't try to reclaim my body so soon. I need to be broken in first.

Still, it feels like I'm clinging to a child's prayer more than anything as the woman leaves, gently closing the door behind her.

Soon, another woman enters. The doctor, I assume from her crisp white jacket and studious bun. Without uttering a single word, she gives me a thorough, clinical examination. I shiver as her cold hands prod my inner thighs and healing scars.

Finally, she leaves.

And hopelessness washes over me, so vast and heavy that I'm sure I'll never escape it. Dangerous thoughts feed on the panic. *Do it now. Take the easy way out, like Marnie did.*

I can't go back.

I can't.

I can't.

Enough! I shake myself, lurching to my feet.

If Mischa is alive, I know the first conclusion he'd jump to: that I went back willingly. That I'm lying in Robert's arms right now, laughing over the idiocy of the monster who deigned to show me a glimpse that he might be something more.

He'd be smug, Mischa, the bastard. He wouldn't contemplate for a second that I would be pacing my gilded prison, aching to be anywhere. Dead. With him. Anywhere.

But my brain won't let me take that cowardly outlook for too long. It keeps returning to him. I see his face, those flashing eyes. They offer a challenge: *You want to prove me wrong, Rose? Then fucking run.*

I rush to the door and test the knob. It's locked.

Two windows, shrouded in scarlet curtains, are positioned on either side of the bed. I race toward one and draw the curtains back only to reveal the plywood nailed to it, obscuring any view. The second has been barred the same way.

Two additional doors lead to a closet and the bathroom. Apart from the bed, my only other piece of furniture is the wardrobe.

I'm trapped.

Tears well and escape before I can prevent their fall. I rub at them, but eventually, I wind up on my knees, against the wall, choking back sobs. They rip from me in dizzying waves, leaving my chest aching in the aftermath.

I barely hear the gentle murmur in between my gasping breaths.

"Shhh," a woman urges. "Shhh, love. It's all right. Shhhh. It's all right."

The words aren't directed to me, but that voice…

"Briar?" I whisper, pressing my ear harder to the wall. It must be thin enough that she can hear me, whoever she is. But the voice falls silent.

"Please. Briar, is that you?"

In a room that potentially isn't locked?

Desperate, I risk raising my voice. "Please answer me. Briar… Please."

But no matter how many times I call, she never replies.

When the door to my cell opens again, I'm huddled on the floor, forced to scramble to my feet as Robert enters.

"Good news," he declares, his lips parted in a glorious smile. "The doctor believes your face can be saved."

He pauses and I can't resist habit driven in through years of obedience. Almost without prompting from my brain, my lips pry apart and I croak, "Th-that's wonderful—"

"With a few minor surgeries, you'll be your old self in no time," Robert agrees, still grinning. Then his eyes slide down to observe the rest of my battered limbs and his mouth flattens. "I've brought you something to wear, love."

He's flanked by a maid who approaches the bed and lays a dress across the foot of it. It's blue, made of silk, perfectly tailored. One of mine, I suspect, taken from my old wardrobe.

But I know for certain we aren't at Winthorp Manor.

"Leave us," Robert snaps at the woman, who scurries away.

She closes the door with a soft thud and my courage dies with it.

"My darling…"

I'm frozen as he advances and smooths his hands down my newly washed shoulders. For what feels like an eternity, his gaze roves from my injured face downward. With every inch traveled, his eyes narrow further.

In disgust.

I hope so. So fiercely that it hurts. He'll storm away and let me heal, too repulsed to try to reclaim what another monster has already messed over. I barely recognize the battered, bruised limbs revealed beneath the ivory cotton.

But then he fingers a lock of my hair, twisting the gleaming strands.

"You're still so beautiful." He sounds surprised by that fact. His flared nostrils inhale the air and his eyes flutter shut as he processes my scent. "I've missed you. The thought of you in that place…" He opens his eyes and I'm shocked to find that they're watering. Clearing his throat, he shakes his head and gently caresses my cheek. "It doesn't matter. You're safe now."

Safe. That word circles my skull as I resist the urge to cringe from his touch. It's such a vicious taunt. *Safe. Safe. Safe.*

"I will never let you go again," he swears.

My spine goes rigid when he leans in, but all he does is press his mouth across my jaw. Cold lips linger over Mischa's brand, imparting a sting I haven't felt since the wounds were freshly carved there.

"I'm sorry," he breathes against the scars. "I don't know how that little bitch—" Breaking off, he glowers at the wall. "Just know that I never intended for *you* to be hurt."

"Briar," I guess, treating her name with all the care of a live grenade. "Is she alive?"

"For now." His callous shrug catches me off guard. He and his sister had their own twisted rivalry, but I've never heard him refer to her so coldly before. "You don't have to worry about her. She's somewhere where she can't meddle, the little cunt. I don't know how she knew… It doesn't matter. She couldn't gloat for long."

But I remember her face as she appeared in the woods. My proud sister didn't look devious or triumphant then. She looked terrified.

"I have something for you." Robert returns his attention to me, placing his hand on my shoulder. "Something I should have returned to you a long time ago… What is this?" He swipes his finger along my throat and I don't register reaching up to stop him.

The necklace. That was what I was trying to protect. I realize that belatedly as white spots explode over my vision, and I regain awareness on my knees, tasting blood.

"I'm sorry. I'm *sorry*," Robert hisses as he and the rest of the room fade in and out of focus.

Dazed, I watch him shake out the fingers of his right hand and rub at the knuckles.

"I'm sorry. But why did you make me—do you realize what I've gone through without you? And this?" He brandishes a delicate chain between his fingers. My necklace. He must have torn it off, the source of his ire. "What the fuck is this?"

"Robert…" A sharp pain makes me swipe my hand across my mouth. In shock, I gape as my fingers come away red— an accessory as familiar to me as the dress on the bed is. Both compose my costume: a battered, caged bird.

"What?" he snarls, rounding on my position.

"It's my mother's," I murmur awkwardly while more liquid drips down my chin. "The necklace. I think it was my mother's—"

"She's dead," he snaps. Then he blinks and shakes his head, tucking the chain into his pocket. "I'll get you a new one, love. Would you like that? Something prettier."

A beautiful collar.

"But this? The fucking woman should have taken it. I'll have her beaten for this." He starts to pace, still muttering. "I don't want anything to remind you of that degenerate. He's fucked you, hasn't he?" His sharp bark of laughter chills my blood. "Of course he has. It's okay. I forgive you.

You survived and you're back now. You're safe. No one else will ever have you."

As his eyes glow a poisonous brown, all doubt is stripped away. *This* is the man I know.

Dread solidifies in my stomach, and nothing is clearer: If I stay in this cage, I'll never leave it again.

There is only one way out. It's the same dilemma I faced when assaulted by Nikolaus, and the tactic I used then is my weapon now.

Rebellion.

"Let me go."

He stiffens, frowning in confusion. "What did you say?"

I swallow, sensing the danger building in his narrow frame. His fingers flex, already reddening from his previous strike. "Just let me go," I whisper, cradling my throbbing jaw. "I can't live like this. Just let me go…"

"Go?" Uncertainty disrupts his rage. He almost resembles the boy he was what seems like a lifetime ago, mulling over the best way to get his point across to my ignorant brain. "Back to him?"

"Anywhere," I rasp. "I can't live like this anymore—"

"He's brainwashed you." He shakes his head, his expression crestfallen. "My sweet Elle—"

"No!" I meet his gaze, imploring him to listen. "I'm not brainwashed. I'm not broken. And he may be a degenerate, but at least… He knows what he is. And his name is Mischa—"

Bam! A monstrous crash resonates through the wall. From the other room.

"Fuck." Robert flushes red and I'm instantly forgotten. "That dumb bitch."

Whirling on his heel, he throws the door open and storms into the hall. I hear the click of another door opening nearby. The room beside mine?

"I'm sorry," a woman pleads a second later, but her voice is higher than Briar's could ever be. Plaintive. "It just fell. I'll clean it up—"

A sharp thwack muffles her cry.

"Can you not serve one goddamn purpose?" Robert hisses. I can picture him towering above a cowering figure as he wipes his stinging hand on the front of his suit. "You've ruined everything. Maybe I should sell you now? What else are you good for?"

The woman mumbles something unintelligible and another slap cuts her off.

"Enough," Robert bellows. "We'll return to the manor tonight and I will hire your replacement—"

"Please," the woman begs. "Not…not in front of him."

Him. Another man?

No. Those cries weren't hers I realize. They were too soft. Too high-pitched.

"*He* will learn," Robert snarls. "You see this woman? She is replaceable."

As he rages, I finally notice that the door to my room is open.

I could run. I *am*, staggering to my feet, lunging toward the doorway.

But I'm too late.

Robert appears before me, his expression flickering as he takes in my breathless stance paces from freedom.

Beyond him, a lush, carpeted hallway extends out of my view.

"You need more rest," Robert says while reaching for the doorknob. "Once we're home… Everything will be as it was. I promise." He smooths his hand over my cheek.

Then he leaves.

And I break.

I'm too hollow for tears. All I can do is breathe raggedly, my face pressed against the floor. Faint cries still emanate from the other room, echoing mine and cementing the chilling reality.

I'll never leave.

And even if Mischa comes after me, with Robert's resources, he would never make it through the front door.

"Shhh," the woman in the other room soothes. "Shhh. Please hush, my darling."

"Ama," the softer voice wails in response.

Who are they? *Mafiya* captives? New additions to his supposed sex trade?

Crawling to the wall, I rap my knuckles against it. "Ama?" I call tentatively. "Is that your name?"

Both figures fall silent.

"Please." Biting my lip, I try again, knocking even louder. "Answer me, please. I won't hurt you—"

"He'll hear you," the woman whispers frantically. "His spies are always listening."

My fingers tremble, leaving streaks of sweat over the wallpaper. Despite everything, one fact strikes me more than any other. I've dealt with plenty of Robert's favorite maids and whores—but she sounds like...*me.*

Her fear. The hitch in her voice. Those subtle clues prove to me that she isn't some recent captive. No, she's been under his thumb for much longer.

"We need to leave," I risk whispering. "I can't stay here. I won't."

I shut my eyes against a telltale burn, keeping any tears at bay.

"Do you know where we are?" I ask.

Silence.

Gritting my teeth in frustration, I turn from the wall and brace my back against it. "I can't stay here," I repeat, though more to myself than anyone else. "I'd rather die than stay here. I'll die…"

There are a multitude of ways I could usher along that inevitable ending. The bathtub would be the easiest option. I'd only need to find something sharp. It's Marnie's method, but maybe I finally understand how she must have felt. This oppressive, suffocating need to run.

I can't stay here.

"Hotel."

"What?" I turn to the wall again, pressing my ear against it so tightly that it hurts. "What did you say?"

"We're in a hotel," the woman replies hoarsely. "I think so… But an old one. One he owns. It's in the middle of nowhere. The windows are locked. There are guards in front of every door. There is no escape."

No… I squeeze my eyes shut and dig my nails into my palms so viciously that I break the skin. No escape.

Is that so? Mischa would taunt were he here. *You're just taking the easy fucking way out. You want to stay with him. Admit it.*

"Never," I snarl out loud. I sound insane—but it's all I have. Arguing with a phantom.

Helpless, I eye the ceiling and another grim plan forms: a makeshift rope with the bedsheets tied to a sturdy post. Hanging. Could I do it? In my morbid search, my eyes keep returning to a unique square-shaped cut-out closed off with metal slats.

A vent.

Cautiously, I lurch to my feet. Without something to climb on, it's too far out of my reach, and the wardrobe towers too high to stand on. Frantic, I race toward the bed, but the frame is solid wood, impossible to budge.

"Hello," I call to the other woman. "Is there a vent in your ceiling?"

"Yes," she whispers back. "But I can't reach it."

"Damn it." I fight against the panic building in my skull, warning me that it's futile. *Just give in.* "Is there anything heavy in your room? A table? Anything you can move or stand on?"

I hear a scraping sound like someone rising to their feet. Then soft, hesitant footsteps. Finally, I sense her return to the wall.

"Yes," she says. "There is a table."

"Good." It takes everything I have to keep my building hope from my voice. "If you stand on it, do you think you can reach the vent?"

More silence.

"Yes," she says nearly a minute later. "I…I think so."

"Thank God." I swallow hard, knowing that what I'm asking is more than anyone ever should of a stranger. But this isn't the time for pleasantries. "I need you to climb into the vent, Ama. If you come to my room, you can open mine. If you can bring me a sheet, anything like a rope, then I can climb. We can leave."

It's far-fetched. I know that even as the plan leaves my mouth. Far-fetched. Stupid. Futile.

But it's all I have.

"If we can make it out—no. I *know* we can make it. I know we can."

I hear nothing from the other end, but for good, I suspect. Ama's stopped listening.

But I can't stop talking.

"He'll kill you," I tell her. "He'll kill me too."

One day, eventually. I know as much with a certainty even Mischa's madness couldn't inspire.

"But I can't stay here. Not anymore. And you have a child with you?"

I hear a sharp intake of air.

"Yes," she admits.

"Then please…"

Silence falls again and I'm too tired to make another attempt. Instead, I curl onto my side and will my conscious mind far away.

It turns to Mischa, a fitting tool to compound on Robert's prison; before he can do it, I'll drive myself insane.

I can feel him inside me, my own devious, maddening parasite. *Is this how it ends, Little Rose?* he taunts. *With you on your knees, too pathetic to run? No. Get the fuck up. Try again. Run!*

Gasping, I pull myself upright, clinging to the wall for balance. My first few steps carry me in a pathetic circle. Then farther. Faster. Feeling along the walls, I test for any breaks. When that fails, I try moving the bed again. Then I retest the windows, running my fingers along the impenetrable wood. Still, I keep moving. Thinking. Trying —anything.

Everything.

I'll give in by the end. Robert will come for me before dawn. I know it.

But still, I resist the inevitable for as long as I can, even if it hurts.

Even if it leaves me too tired to fight back when my captor returns. Even if it leaves me exhausted and panting, I keep trying.

Eventually, I sink onto the bed, my face in my hands. Winthorp Manor looms, my virtual gallows. Once I enter beyond those gleaming walls, I know I'll never come back out. At least not as the woman I am now—Mischa's spiteful Little Rose.

Something tickles my nose and I jolt to awareness. There's no one around. My door is still closed, but cool air ruffles my hair…

Coming from above.

"Please hurry," a soft voice calls.

Looking up, I see the vent hanging open and a pale hand reaching from beyond like the madness only possible in a dream.

"All I have is a sheet," my rescuer says weakly. "It's secured to my waist, but you need to climb quickly."

As I gape, a tightly curled strip of ivory descends from the darkness.

I don't hesitate to grab it. But within seconds, I realize the full daunting nature of what my reckless planning requires.

I'm still physically weak, healing from multiple fractures and a severed finger. Climbing at all is hard—but without Mischa's ruthless strength to spur me on, it's damn near impossible. My feet dangle helplessly, inches off the ground.

It's hopeless…

Enough! I shake my head to clear it and reach higher. Then higher. Sweat beads on my forehead and pours down my shoulders, slicking my nightgown to my flesh. I'm moving too slowly. Any minute, Robert will return and this will all be in vain.

Fear of that outcome spurs me faster even as my muscles scream in protest. Closing my eyes, I focus on inching higher despite the searing pain. Higher. Finally, I lift my hand and my fingers strike a firm surface.

"I'll help you," Ama whispers and her hands grab mine. It's a struggle to pull myself the final distance, but finally, I'm fully inside the vent, panting on the frigid metal.

"We need to move," I say as Ama wrestles the vent closed after me.

She's pale up close, with long, dark hair shrouding her lithe frame. Behind her, an even smaller figure huddles out of sight.

"I don't think these extend far," she whispers. "They might be able to hear us through them."

My blood runs cold at the thought. *This is insane,* a part of me insists. I should climb down. Wait for Robert. If he finds us now, it will be so much worse.

"I think we can go this way." Ama tugs my hand and shuffles forward.

I follow, suppressing a cough as dust and grime catch beneath my fingers. I don't know how far we go before she reaches back.

"It's a dead end." Her voice shakes, racked with terror. "We have to go down."

Down leads into darkness glimpsed only through the slats of another vent.

"I'll go first." I lift the grate and reach for the coiled sheet still trailing from Ama's waist.

"I'm okay," she whispers as I hesitate. "Just…hurry."

I climb down, suppressing a groan as my muscles strain, pushed to their limit. Feet from the floor, my arms give way and I drop down, landing hard.

Bang! The solid thud echoes as my heart stops. Any moment, Robert or one of his men will come rushing. Seconds pass as the air sticks in my lungs.

But no one comes. Yet.

Scrambling upright, I race to get my bearings. Smooth tile flooring betrays that this isn't one of Robert's suites. Faint light enters from a single window, providing just enough context to the shadows to make out where we are: a room filled with towering metal squares stacked one on top of the other.

A laundry room?

"Is it safe?" Ama calls from above.

"I…I don't know," I admit. "But we don't have a choice."

I can sense her wrestling with the same indecision plaguing me. Finally, she sighs.

"I need to send my child down first." Fear distorts her voice, even more pronounced. Her child. She may as well have said her *life*.

"Okay. It's okay." I position myself beneath the vent and raise my arms. "You can lower him down."

Pale limbs pierce the dark, lowered with the utmost care. Ama's son is a thin, wiry boy with a mop of wild, blond hair obscuring delicate features. He stares down on me warily, his eyes massive in the dark.

"Do you have him? Please! Do you have him?"

"Y-yes," I croak, jolting back to awareness. As the child is lowered by his hands, I grab a metal folding chair and stand on it, grabbing him by the waist. Tiny hands paw at my shoulders, gripping tight until I climb from the chair and set him down.

By the time I look up, a slender woman has already unfurled herself from the ceiling to balance precariously on the edge of the chair. Observing her in shadow, I first think she's beautiful. Alarmingly so. Dark hair hangs down to her waist, shrouding a slight frame covered only in a thin, gray dress.

In contrast, the boy is wearing a crisp white shirt and pants that I can tell even in the dark are of expensive quality. He must be the relative of a Winthorp associate. One of Robert's business partners, maybe? The moment his mother descends from the chair, he races to her. "Ama!"

She lifts him, clutching him to her chest. "Now what do we do?" she asks, her face stricken with panic.

"We..." I scan the room and spot a door left ajar at the other end of it. A faint strip of light illuminates potential freedom. "We keep moving," I say, leading the way toward it. "We can't stop now."

I would say that my life has been devoid of anything resembling luck thus far. Maybe the fates have finally smiled upon me, because beyond the laundry room, we find a stairwell extending down.

I lead the way, my heart in my throat, but at the base of the steps, propped open with a cinder block, is yet another door.

Fresh air tickles my nose, acrid and heavy—but it's too good to be true. I know that even before I hear the low, grating hum of a man whistling nearby.

"Shhh," I hiss to Ama, who goes still on the bottom step.

Inching forward along the wall, I spot the culprit of the sound. He's leaning against the outside of the building, blowing cigarette smoke into the open air. Dressed in a bulky shirt and jeans, he doesn't seem like one of Robert's men. A worker of this building perhaps?

I scan him more intently, deciphering what little clues I can. The sleeves of his shirt are rolled up enough to reveal a tattoo on his forearm: a gyrating serpent intertwined with a cross.

Frantic, Ama paws at my shoulder. "There's someone there," she breathes against my ear. "What now?"

My eyes go to the makeshift doorjamb, and once again, I channel Mischa. What was it he told Mouse? *You can't hesitate.*

"Wait!" Ama gasps as I slink forward. "What are you doing?"

I'm not sure. I can't let myself think it through, either. Quietly, I stoop for the brick and replace it with my bare foot. My leg trembles, fighting to support the door's weight as I lift the brick as high as I can—which is mere inches from the ground.

You want to die a pathetic little bitch? my imaginary Mischa goads. *Then go back. Let him inside you again. Be his whore again. His wife. His toy.*

Inhaling sharply, I force myself to focus. Luckily, the man isn't paying the doorway any attention. He doesn't see me creep between the sliver of open space, hefting the brick even higher. A single question crosses my mind: Could I really hit a stranger?

Kill him?

Yes...

No?

But as Ama said, Robert owns this building. Anyone here works first and foremost for him and the Winthorps. So I shut off the part of my brain urging me to retreat and count to three.

One…

Two…

Just as I tense to spring forward, the man turns and strolls up a concrete path in the opposite direction, still whistling. I give myself only seconds to recognize the change in fate before I shoulder the door open fully and beckon Ama through it.

The bracing night air greets us like a slap, cold and unforgiving. My bare feet register hard pavement beneath them, and the only real source of light comes from an orange bulb jutting above the door.

At least the man is gone from view—for now.

Beyond the narrow exit, a parking lot stretches across the entire width of a massive brick building. As Ama claimed, it's grand enough to be a hotel—but a reclusive one, used only by the Winthorps, I suspect.

Looming shapes betray a few vehicles. The nearest one is a massive white van. It's only as I race toward it that I realize I still have the brick in my grasp. In the darkness, I notice Ama eyeing it, and she clutches her son even tighter to her chest.

"Shh, my darling," she soothes as he starts to whimper. "Shh… Everything is fine—"

"We have to get out of here." I approach the van and tug on the first door I can reach. "Shit!"

It's locked. Just as I spot a car a few yards away, that guttural whistle returns.

"Damn it," I hiss. "We need to find—"

"Over here." Ama waves frantically from the other side of the van. "I think I've opened it!"

Sure enough, I circle around and find her propping open the door to the front seat with her hip.

"Thank God!" I slam the button on the console to unlock the rest. "Get in."

"Can you drive?" the woman asks fearfully as I claim the driver's seat.

I don't answer her. Once again, fate has chosen to both mock and reward me. The owner of this vehicle left the keys in the ignition.

As well as a knife on the passenger's seat.

A reddish liquid paints the surface and my stomach churns. I wrench the glove compartment open and find a wad of tissues, which I toss over the weapon for the child's sake.

Then I palm the steering wheel and try to breathe.

"Hold on," I warn as I rack my brain for every lesson Mischa taught me. Brake, I recall, identifying that particular pedal. Gas.

After that? Hope and prayer.

"I can do this," I murmur. Then I glance in the rearview mirror and my blood runs cold.

The smoking man has returned. Only now, he stands awkwardly, his neck craned, his hand positioned over his eyes like a visor as he stares in our direction.

"Oh God," Ama chokes out. "He'll spot us soon, if he hasn't already."

"We're fine," I insist.

But there isn't even time to panic.

Aiming my gaze on a clear path through the lot, I twist the key and slam on the gas. The van jerks beneath me, a living, untamable thing. I have to throw myself against the steering wheel to narrowly avoid hitting another vehicle.

"Careful!" Ama cries. "Please…"

Mingled with her voice is a softer whine that tugs at my heart.

"It's fine," I rasp.

Fortunately, the parking lot is surrounded by a stretch of desolate fields, and in the distance, a lone road leads to the horizon. I don't recognize this area—which only reinforces the fact that I barely know a world beyond Winthorp Manor.

I could be leading us to a dead end. A river. A lake. A cliff.

For a second, I can't suppress that panicked, pathetic part of me Robert Winthorp nurtured for so damn long.

What am I doing? I should return. Give in. Surrender.

But Mischa's voice is louder, drowning out all other thoughts in my head.

Run, Little Rose. Fucking run.

I drive for hours until the van slows to a crawl despite how hard I slam on the gas pedal. A straining groan issues from the engine with every attempt.

"We're out of petrol," Ama points out, her voice thin. Around a yawn, she warns, "We won't make it far on foot."

She sounds more realistic than pessimistic, but the point is the same: Without the van, it's only a matter of time until we wind up caught in the net of one monster or the other.

Suspiciously, I don't think we've been followed. Yet.

"They must not have noticed we're gone," Ama says as if reading my mind. I glance back and find her staring pensively from the window, stroking her son's hair. "But not for long."

I copy her, unnerved by the lightening sky. Eventually, I have no choice but to pull over onto the side of the road before the engine dies altogether. The surrounding countryside is eerily empty—something that I doubt is a regular occurrence.

Robert is powerful enough to keep certain roads clear at his leisure. All it takes is money pressed into the right hands to have traffic temporarily diverted, robbing us of any helpful passerby.

And blocking off the route of any potential rescue from a certain *mafiya* leader in the process.

"We can't stay here." I shoulder the door open on my end and step out onto shockingly cold gravel. A chilling breeze cuts through the thin fabric of my nightgown and reinforces the fact that I'm barefoot.

So are Ama and her son.

Just how far will we make it like this? Biting my lip, I smother the thought.

"Come on. We need to keep moving." I reach back into the van and grab the knife, holding it awkwardly in my damaged hand.

"We're ready." Ama moves stiffly, never letting go of her son for a second. Once out of the van, she faces me. "Where will we go…" She trails off, her eyes wide as she takes me in in the full light of day.

I know I'm staring at her as well.

She's alarmingly pale. So pale that she glows, but the pallor just enhances her beauty. And her smooth, unblemished skin only serves as a harsh contrast to mine: sliced and bruised and swollen.

"I don't know," I say as I turn away, shrouding as much of my face as I can behind my uninjured hand. "Come. Let's go."

"Ama!"

I look back and find the boy squirming in her arms.

"It's her," he says, pointing at me. His other hand claws at his neck and tugs a necklace from beneath the collar of his shirt. It's beautiful, if simple: a slender gold chain supporting a square-shaped charm. "The angel—"

"Hush, my darling." Ama turns his face toward her chest and shushes him until he goes silent.

My cheeks heat as I turn toward a swath of trees—the only coverage in view—and start walking, wincing as the uneven terrain tears at my bare heels. In theory, two women and a child shouldn't go far without being recaptured.

But, somehow, we reach the edge of the forest unaccosted. From there, it's a slow, painful trek toward nowhere. Brambles claw at my skin. Holding the knife, I'm weighed down as much as Ama. My exhausted, broken body can only go so far before my legs threaten to give out entirely.

"We…need…rest," Ama croaks in between panting breaths. Her arms quiver as she readjusts the boy on her hip. "Just for a moment—"

"We can't," I insist, even as my trembling hand clings to a nearby branch for balance. I feel it in the pit of my soul: If we stop now, it's over. "They've had nearly a day to hunt us down."

As I retrace our steps in my head, I realize how pathetically little we've traveled overall. Finding us will be child's play if they aren't encroaching on our position already.

And, God, I can sense them now: specters in every flickering shadow and rustling of distant leaves. I tighten my grip on the knife as much as possible, but with as weak as I am, I can barely brandish it higher than my knee.

Still, I stagger forward, grasping for another tree or branch. "We can't stop moving—"

"Someone's coming!" Ama cries.

Panic surges up my throat, robbing my voice, as my straining ears catch the same sound: the telltale crunch of footsteps expertly traversing the underbrush.

"N-no." Moisture floods my eyes, and it takes every ounce of strength I can muster to blink back the forming tears. "Hide," I spit toward Ama, but I don't check to see if she obeys.

Instead, I shift my focus toward putting as much distance between us as possible—and making as much noise as I can in the process.

I'll die rather than go back to Robert, but maybe I can ensure that I'm the only one forced to choose that fate.

And it seems our pursuer has taken the bait. His footsteps advance on me rapidly, growing less stealthy the closer he comes. Soon, I can hear him breathing. Panting.

I wait until I assume he's close enough to grab me. Then I pivot, lashing out with the knife. "Stay away from me!"

He grunts in shock, narrowly avoiding the blade. Then he grabs my arm and the game is over. Iron strength nearly takes me off my feet.

"Do you really think you can stab me, Little Rose?" he hisses.

I look at him sharply and blink. My eyes are playing tricks. Or maybe he's a joke conjured by delirium.

The figure before me certainly could be such a specter: a haggard-looking Mischa, his chin covered in stubble. His bloodshot eyes are honed like lasers, taking in my thin, beautiful nightgown and coifed hair. He opens his mouth, presumably to say something. A quip?

But I'm too tired to hear it.

"Mischa!" I throw myself toward him, and his arms encircle my waist. My face finds the crook of his shoulder and I breathe him in, relishing the heat and the way he stiffens against me—still so fucking suspicious. I can't humor him now. I try to speak, but all I can do is moan and go limp.

Something in my appearance keeps him silent. I'm in his arms within seconds, held tightly to his chest. His heartbeat plays a steady rhythm as he starts to move, racing through the underbrush. It's only now that I remember.

"Wait," I croak, bracing my hand against his shoulder.

"What is it?"

"There's someone else—"

"What?" He cranes his neck back and then goes rigid.

Following the line of his gaze, I see why.

Ama didn't run and hide after all. In the dim light filtering between the trees, she looks almost ethereal, her hair falling like a cloak. Wide-eyed, she gapes at Mischa. Then she sinks to her knees, still clutching her son to her chest. Her pink lips flutter, forming the same sound over and over, but it's wasted seconds before my brain can finally interpret it. A name.

"M-Mischa?"

The arms around me loosen, and I'm forced to stand, clinging to his shoulder for balance.

"No… You're dead." Mischa shakes his head, his expression pained. Broken. "No… *Anna?*"

"Oh my God!" Tears stream down Ama's face as she rocks herself, clinging to her son so tightly that the boy whines in response. "Mischa!"

He advances on her with slow, deliberate steps. Then, suddenly, he's on his knees, his arms thrown around her.

"Anna," he mutters. "I can't believe it. Anna."

And something pangs in my chest, so subtle that I barely register it before the feeling spreads, blossoming into full-blown shock that brings me to my knees.

Anna. Anna-*Natalia*.

His Anna.

She's alive.

CHAPTER 10

Their reunion lasts for only a second before Mischa reluctantly stands and helps Anna to her feet.

"We need to move," he warns. But one look at her trembling body and his jaw clenches.

I was so focused on myself, but I wasn't the only one expending every ounce of strength I have. Her knees wobble, threatening to buckle any second. From her arms, the boy stares fearfully.

It's a miracle we came this far.

"Carry her," I tell Mischa. "I can take the baby—"

"No!" Anna hugs the boy to her, heedless of his plaintive cries. "I can keep moving. I can—"

"There's no time. Here—give him to me." Mischa reaches for the boy and Anna finally relinquishes him. Effortlessly,

Mischa swings the child around, setting him on his back. "Grab my neck," he commands, guiding the boy's tiny hands into position. "But don't you dare choke me."

Before Anna can protest, she's in his arms as well.

Meeting my gaze, Mischa inclines his head. "My men aren't far, but we need to run. Do you understand, Rose?"

I nod, and then he's gone at a lightning pace, picking through the underbrush with enviable grace. My lungs churn fire as I follow clumsily in his wake. There's no space in my exhausted brain left for caution. I throw myself forward without tact, my arms flailing for balance.

I'm loud and bumbling, and worst of all...

I'm slowing him down.

The fact that he's even in my line of sight at all betrays the lengths he's gone through to keep pace with me, despite being encumbered as he is.

"You need to keep moving, Little Rose," he taunts from up ahead, his breathing heavy. "Don't you fucking dare slow down. Stay with me... Stay with me!"

"I'm...trying..." It's a lie. Every last bit of energy I had has already been expended. Pure momentum drives me now. I'm losing speed, falling farther and farther behind. He's merely a speck now, bobbing on the horizon.

Carried by the wind, his voice reaches me. "Don't you dare give up. Move! Or do you *want* to get captured?"

Bastard. I keep going, if only out of spite. Gradually, his distant shape grows larger. Am I hallucinating?

No…

He's stopped.

Gasping, I scan our surroundings and realize why; we've finally reached a break in the woods. Up ahead, the trees give way to a narrow field marred by tire tracks.

"What now?" I croak to Mischa.

He pays me no mind. Stepping forward, he bellows over the landscape, "To me!"

As if on cue, several men rush forward to meet us from the underbrush. Their trademark fatigues reveal their identity: the *mafiya.*

One of them grabs Anna while another races toward me. Seconds later, I find myself in a van, hurtling toward an unknown destination.

"Where are we?" I manage to croak.

"Heading east," a man replies from the front seat. "We'll be in Sergei's territory soon."

Three others crowd the enclosed space alongside me, including the driver, their faces stern and focused on the road. I don't recognize a familiar figure among them—not even Vanya.

"Where is Mischa?" I ask, peering through the nearest window. Just behind this vehicle, I can make out the looming shape of another van.

Mischa, Anna, and the boy must be in another vehicle altogether.

Because otherwise…I'm alone.

*D*arkness shrouds the interior of the van when it finally comes to an abrupt stop. Consciousness is a battle I've fought to the bitter end. By now, my bloodshot eyes can barely open wide enough to make out my surroundings. Beyond the van, the vague outline of a structure looms, ghosted by moonlight.

Could it be Winthorp Manor?

Or was my escape more than a fantastical dream?

"Stay with me, Little Rose."

I jump as someone opens the door on my side. Cool air spills in and I find myself in familiar arms without warning.

"I've got you."

My head lolls against a muscled shoulder, a stern jaw the only focal point I can fixate on. God, he looks older, aged overnight. From this angle, the shadows beneath his eyes hollow his features, more defined than ever.

"Am I safe?" I ask, my voice a broken whisper. Despite everything, I'm curious as to his answer. Will he make the same boast Robert did once his pawn was back within his possession? *Safe. Safe. Safe.*

I wait for a mocking taunt, but he says nothing else as he carries me toward a grand structure that, at a glance, I can tell dwarfs even his old manor in comparison.

Sergei's property?

It's made of stone, at least four stories tall. The layout isn't as flashy as that of Winthorp Manor's. Regal and modest, it's more enclosed: a family home rather than a status symbol.

In the fading light, I make out a paved courtyard containing a small garden casting a mockingly sweet aroma as we pass. Up ahead, a massive door opens and from it rushes Vanya.

"Thank God," he says, spotting us. "You found her—"

"Papa?"

That voice stops him dead in his tracks, and I fear he'll collapse. Wildly, he scans the area before his gaze finally fixates on something beyond us.

"No," he croaks, his voice rasping. "No, it can't be..."

A hesitant step propels him down the stone path. Then another, until he's running across the courtyard. I turn in time to catch a slender figure limping toward him.

"Papa!" Instantly, she's engulfed in his arms and they sink to their knees, heedless of the paved stone beneath them. It's too raw of a moment to ogle for long. Too intimate.

I turn away, surprised to find Mischa staring resolutely ahead as well. Once we reach the entrance to the manor, he carries me into the grand foyer beyond it. Here, the mood shifts entirely as we're approached by a watchful Sergei.

"You found her," the older man says, eyeing me with a terse nod. "How?"

"Ask her," Mischa says, jostling me in his arms. "In fact, how fucking useful are you and your so-called expert intel?"

"Something happened." Sergei's eyes narrow imperceptibly. "Explain."

"No. How about you explain?" Mischa stops short of running into the other man altogether—for my sake, I suspect.

Trapped between them, I'm the only one who would suffer.

"For one," Mischa continues, "explain why, despite all your intel on the Winthorps, you've never mentioned that your *real* niece was alive?"

Sergei frowns. "What are you…" Then he turns to the commotion in the courtyard and something flits across his face so quickly that I can barely trace it. Shock?

Before I can be sure, he's already halfway to his brother and his niece.

"I thought you were dead," I admit to Mischa. I'm still in his arms, in a hallway, I think. Then a room. "I thought—"

"You need to sleep," he says, lowering me to a soft surface I assume to be a bed.

From the corner of my eye, I notice emerald-green walls, and a lavish canopy shrouds me from above.

"Go ahead," Mischa commands. "Get some rest. I'll be here."

"Oh?" A tired laugh trickles from my throat, much to my surprise. "To make sure I don't run away?"

Of all the times to joke…

This one lands flat.

"Yes." He scans my face, hunting for something. Searching. As my eyes drift shut, I hear him mutter, "Though maybe you shouldn't have come back after all, Little Rose. Maybe you shouldn't have come back…"

I wake up, aware of nothing other than the fact that I'm alone—and the most selfish, pathetic thought crosses my mind before I can squash it.

I want it to have been a dream: Robert. Anna.

Everything.

I want to wake up to an infuriated Mischa glaring over me while Vanya lurks worriedly in the next room and Mouse skips down the hall.

Seeing Robert at all, and finding Anna-Natalia, could have been just some vivid nightmare…

But I feel it: a cold sense of dread congealing in my belly like a lead weight. Something vital has changed. Positions have been altered overnight and nothing will be as it was.

I try to evade the inevitable by lying beneath the blankets for as long as I can. They're expensive quality, like the kind in Mischa's manor. The glimpses I have of the room as I toss and turn reveal an elegant, yet comfortable space with dark-green wallpaper and hardwood floors.

My bed is massive, shielded by a heavy, embroidered canopy: silver vines sewn over a rich forest green. When I finally shrug the blankets off and sit upright, I spot a set of neatly folded clothing on a polished wooden dresser in the corner. Across from it, a heavy chair is positioned near a wide window overlooking an expansive view of tailored gardens.

"We will regroup at my property," Sergei said what feels like an eternity ago. So this must be the place.

A world where Mischa Stepanov doesn't hold sway.

He didn't even keep his promise to watch over me. Straining my ears, I don't hear him grumbling or shouting nearby, either.

Cautiously, I try to stand only to gasp as pain ripples through my spine. Everything, down to my toes, throbs at the slightest attempt to bear any weight. I'm covered in thin scratches as well, though I don't need to look any farther than my torn, bleeding feet to know that I've pushed my body to its limits.

But the longer I stay in bed, the more that ominous dread in my gut grows. Limping to the dresser is the only way to push back that reality for as long as possible. The clothing I find is a pink dress with long sleeves. Courtesy of Mischa?

I picture him finding the garment he'd consider the most insulting. Robert's precious wife bundled in pink after being pried from his grasping hands. How ironic would that be?

I can't even look at the color without shuddering, so I set the garment aside and bite my pride back enough to open a drawer and snatch something new from it: another dress in a shade of blue.

Sergei keeps his home well stocked, it seems.

My search of the room thankfully turns up an en suite bathroom equipped with a tub large enough to submerge myself in completely. I run the water as hot as I can stand it and climb in. Washing Robert away a second time is a grueling, tenuous affair.

My battered limbs take ages to scrub clean. Once I've dried off and wrapped in a towel, I brush my teeth until my gums bleed. Then I use a bit of hand soap for good measure.

Dramatic in a sense. Or perhaps poetic?

He doesn't own me anymore.

But who does? When I finally gather the nerve to creep from my room, I feel rudderless. A careening ship without a captain, barely able to avoid the rocks waiting to dash me to pieces.

And this new landscape seems to contain plenty of pitfalls to stumble upon.

Sergei's home is a maze of ornate hallways, much like Mischa's Pecavi—only this place feels older. Colder.

Prestige seems printed into the very wallpaper and embedded in every portrait of a nameless figure I pass. A modest color scheme of dark green and silver creates a quiet atmosphere.

So quiet.

My footsteps echo, jarringly loud. Any minute, a snarling *mafiya* leader should appear from around a corner and snidely insinuate I have ulterior motives.

By the time I reach a grand, circular staircase, I've found no one. Here, at least, voices drift from nearby. I follow them to a small sitting room.

Inside it, Vanya is sitting on a leather chair, angled toward Anna. She's been washed and dressed in a clean black dress. In her arms, her son sleeps, held to her chest as she and her father speak in low, hushed tones. Suddenly, he reaches out, bracing his hand on her knee, and I can make out the glint of tears painting her cheeks.

Quietly, I turn away and continue past them. I have no idea how long this hallway goes or where it travels. Almost in a daze, I turn a corner and nearly trip over a small body huddled by the wall. Alarm lances down my spine and I jolt back reflexively, my arm outstretched.

But then I make out the figure's pale-blond hair and crouch beside her. "Mouse?"

She turns away from me. Her slight body heaves and she tries to shield her face with one of her hands.

"What's wrong?" A million horrific scenarios march through my mind. So many dark, twisted things.

She shakes her head. Then she brandishes her other hand, holding the trembling fingers up for me to make out the red substance painting each fingertip.

"Oh God. What happened?" I lurch to my feet, my heart racing. Is another attack imminent? "Is it your shoulder?" I ask her out loud. "We need to find Mischa—"

Mouse grabs my hand and tugs before I can take a step. *No!* She points to her belly and it takes my brain a second to put the pieces together.

"How old are you?" I ask, returning to a crouch.

She eyes me warily, mistrust glinting in her green irises. Only God knows how long she's had to survive like this, always on guard.

Finally, she raises all ten of her fingers. Then two.

"Twelve," I say, nodding. "All right. Come with me."

I don't know how to navigate back to my room, but with luck, I find a bathroom nearby and coax her into a shower. The brief looks I get of her body make my heart ache. She's twelve with the physique of a much younger child, though I doubt through natural means. How long has she been deprived of food, or comfort, or basic care?

"You don't have to be embarrassed," I tell her as she huddles at the back of the shower, hunched away from me. "This happens to every woman. My first time, I thought I was dying, but one of the older maids took pity on me and taught me about womanhood."

In crude, explicit terms, but it was a lesson nonetheless.

"You aren't dying," I add as shuffling sounds allude to her studiously scrubbing her body clean. "But you will have to learn to anticipate it. For now, we'll make do, but I'll see if someone can get you proper supplies. Would you like that?"

I pause in the slim chance she'll reply.

"Okay," I say as if she has. "No one else has to know."

Finally, Mouse reemerges, dripping wet. I help her dry off and then I leave her long enough to retrace my steps to the room I woke up in and retrieve the pink dress.

I return and find her rooted firmly where I left her, by the tub. Once she eyes the garment in my hands, she frowns and shakes her head.

"It's just for now," I insist, helping her put it on. "I'm sure you'll be back to climbing trees in no time."

Her wrinkled nose reveals her doubts about that.

When we finally leave the bathroom, she stays close to my side like a shadow. Hiding?

"We should find your room," I suggest. "Do you remember where it—"

"Here you are. The Mouse and Rose." Mischa seems to appear from the very shadows. He's still wearing a pair of filthy, faded fatigues. Either he's gone out again or he's still on guard, unable to relax even here. His eyes scan me in a ruthless sweep, settling on my face, then my hair. "You and I need to have a chat, Rose," he says, his voice uncharacteristically stern. "Preferably now."

"No." I have to clear my throat to find the traction to speak. "I'm tired."

It's like that first day all over again—trapped with him. My initial instinct is to run. I turn on my heel to do just that, but Mouse digs her nails into my wrist and yanks me back. She's surprisingly strong for someone so small. I look down and find her gritting her teeth as she inclines her head down the hall. Apparently, her room is nearby.

"Tired?" Mischa advances a step, his eyes narrowed, and unease washes over me. In an instant, he's switched from playful to guarded as only he can. His jaw twitches as if chewing over the words he plans to say next. Then he shrugs and continues moving, pushing past me. "Suit yourself."

The chill in his voice resonates down to my core. But before it can fully sink in, Mouse tugs me forward and I have no choice but to follow.

Her room is smaller than mine, but not far down. The layout of the floor curves—a giant oval centered around the staircase. Together, Mouse and I find a clean pair of underwear and a maid, who promptly supplies sanitary napkins.

"It should last for seven days or so," I explain as she throws herself onto a modest bed draped in yellow sheets. "The worst thing you'll experience is the cramping. You should learn to anticipate it, trust me. Mine should be due…" I do the math in my head and then bite my lip so hard that it bleeds. "Um…any day now," I croak. "Maybe I'll get to join in your misery?"

I try to smile, but her lips remain resolute in a flat, stubborn line.

"So you are twelve," I say, switching subjects. I wonder if Mischa knew that. Looking at her, I wouldn't guess her any older than nine or ten. "Where are you from?"

She looks away from me, her mouth wrinkling. Then she points to a portrait hanging above the bed.

"The ocean?" I guess, deciphering the clue from the framed scene of a stormy beach.

She shrugs and raises her arm before quickly extending it.

"There was fishing there?" I say, interpreting her miming.

She nods and then returns to her stiff, hunched position, looking at everything but me.

"Can you speak?" I know I'm unwanted here. But maybe she's preferable to the silence and thoughts of Robert and Mischa. Admittedly, a feral dog hungry for my blood would be preferable. "Or do you just choose not to—"

"She can."

I jump as the door opens from the outside, revealing Mischa behind it. He crosses his arms, oblivious as Mouse's cheeks turn blood red.

"How long were you standing there?" I demand.

"The girl can hear, so she isn't mute," he says, shrugging me off. "She can speak, but it's probably painful, and she wouldn't be able to say much, if anything at all. It's a trick that Nicolai uses to silence all of his drug mules. He gives them a daily dose of a chemical cocktail that causes permanent, lasting damage to the vocal cords if taken long enough."

Horror drains any irritation I may feel toward him. "That's horrible—" I break off as Mouse jumps from the bed and storms past Mischa, her hands in fists.

"What's wrong?" He reaches for her arm, but she easily evades him and dashes into the hall. Narrowed, his eyes cut toward me. "What did you say to her?"

"Me?" I scoff. "Maybe she's alarmed by the man who just rudely barged into her room and overheard a private conversation? How much *did* you overhear?"

"I don't know." Mischa frowns, stroking his chin. "Something about fishing."

"What do you know about her?" I blurt, staring at the space she occupied. In so many ways, she seems to fit that stupid nickname. A mysterious, scurrying creature.

"Not much," he admits. "Just what I managed to get out of Nicolai. She was sold to settle a debt."

And he callously threw her into his drug trade.

"Her story isn't as rare as you might think. In fact…" He looks up, meeting my gaze, and alarm jolts down my spine. I step back instinctively, but he's already advancing twice as fast. "Plenty of women find themselves caught up in the schemes of evil men. Isn't that right? Or at least that is the tale they want you to believe…"

He reaches for me, twisting a lock of my hair between his fingers.

"Stop!" I bat his hand away, and he cocks his head as if finally learning the answer to a puzzling question. "You should be with Anna," I croak.

"And where should you be, *Elle*?" he bites back. "How soon before I can expect Robert Winthorp knocking on the front fucking door, following the trail of crumbs you've left for him?"

My hand lashes out with no input from my brain. It's only as I feel the sting through my palm that I realize what I've done: I've slapped him.

And I don't regret one fucking second.

CHAPTER 12

"There she is…" Laughing, he lets the blow glance off him and leans in, forcing me farther into the corner. "What a shame you've dropped your grateful, jail-sprung act so soon. It was almost convincing—"

"And you?" I counter. "You should be with the love of your life, shouldn't you?"

God, I hate how nasty I sound. So damn bitter.

"Though," I choke out as my throat tightens, "maybe you wanted to tie up loose ends first? Don't worry. I can take a hint."

"What the hell are you talking about?"

"What you said," I insist. "According to you…I shouldn't have come back at all."

"What are you—" His eyes narrow and widen in quick succession. Then he laughs. "Oh, Little Rose. The next time you want to overhear my evil musings, maybe you shouldn't fucking pass out before you hear the whole thing? I don't think you should have come back because…"

"What?" I snarl.

"Because—" He grabs my wrist, yanking me against his chest. "Because I don't think I'll be inclined to let you go."

My heart stops. Muttered in such heated tones, the promise should be terrifying. And it is. So many nuances lurk in those words. Things a man like him could never say out loud.

And it's like the exhaustion and pain hit me all at once. I go limp. My arms are the only limbs I have control over and I throw them both around his neck.

"I've got you." He catches me, pinning me against the wall for support. "But if you're trying to choke me, it isn't working."

I'm too exhausted to form a comeback.

I break instead. Tears flood my eyes, and I sob like I never have in my entire life. So many years of pain and torment bleed from me. I can't slow the onslaught. My body trembles in the aftermath, and only now can I finally admit it. I've never been so terrified. So desperate.

I've never fought so damn hard before.

When my sobs finally subside, his fingers creep into my hair, and I finally register his voice murmured insistently into my ear.

"I've got you. I've got you. Let it out. Tell me what happened."

Between gasping pants, I manage to convey everything. The escape. Robert. Everything. But as the words leave my mouth, one thing remains clear: a nagging suspicion I've had since the second I crawled into the damn vent.

"It feels too easy," I admit as I draw back and swipe my hand across my face. "Too…clean."

"Hmm." Mischa strokes his chin, his gaze turned inward. "Like he let you go?"

"No." All I need to do is picture Robert to be sure of that. The man I know would never relinquish his toys, not even for leverage. "More like…"

"What?" His thumb grazes my chin, coaxing an answer from it. I shiver at the contact. Only he could master gentle and demanding in one gesture.

"More like someone planned it?"

But even that sounds too fantastical. The truth could be simpler: Living with Mischa has made me just as paranoid. No wonder he can't help but doubt me. In his world, everyone is an enemy or a potential foe.

Or a weakness waiting to be exploited.

"Anna," I rasp, turning my attention to the view beyond the window. A faint reflection taunts me regardless: his expression, suddenly guarded. "How is she?"

The softness that seeps into his mouth shouldn't make my chest ache. It shouldn't make me instantly scramble several steps away from him. His humanity—as rare as it is—shouldn't send a lance through my heart every bit as alarming as Robert's rage.

"She's..." He looks at the floor. Seconds pass and he can't seem to find a word to describe it: how a woman might feel after years of captivity, only to be miraculously found alive. "I thought she was dead."

Darkness creeps into his expression and just like that, he's hardened Mischa once more.

"They sent her 'body' in pieces. We had a burial. And all this time—" He runs his fingers along the stubble on his chin and sighs. "I said goodbye to her sixteen years ago. But if I knew, even a rumor, I would have broken down their fucking front door."

"I never saw her," I confess. And that's the terrifying thing. For sixteen years, Anna-Natalia was alive, presumably on Winthrop property, and I never saw her. I never heard any of the servants speak of her. Robert never so much as hinted...

And if a man could keep one such secret, only God knows what else he has in store.

"How could I have never seen her?" I'm shaking my head, and more tears threaten to fall. "I never saw her. I never saw—"

"Enough." He steps forward and I marvel at the sensation of being in his arms again. Of all the places in the world to seek refuge, his shoulder shouldn't be my chosen place to find it. I'm a parasite, leeching off his heat—and he lets me feed for as long as I need to.

At least until he wants something from me in return.

"I need to ask it." His fingers fan out down my back, running over the ridges of my spine. "Did he touch you?"

I know what he means. "And if he did?"

"Then he did." His grip tightens the moment I try to pull away. "I'd still want to know."

"Why?" I snarl. "Would that injure your pride? If I had to sleep with him? Would that make you feel like a pathetic, fucking—"

"I'd want to know," he growls into my ear so fiercely that I fall silent. "If he hurt you. If he touched you. I want to know."

"No…" I sigh, too tired to resist him any longer. "He didn't have to."

I felt violated anyway. In his presence, I was old Ellen again, and I know now more than ever that I can never be her. Not anymore.

"Is this the part where you vow to fuck me now?" I wonder, copying his gruff tone. "Erase him? Soothe your own ego?"

"No." His voice is so deep that it resonates in my bones. He isn't taunting me. "This is the part where you listen. To how we were somehow ambushed despite Sergei's protection. How I watched you get taken, and I knew then and there, even if you were a cunning little bitch who went back willingly. Even if it was all a game… Then you would have done your job too well, Rose, because I was going after you."

Only he could make such a heated confession sound more twisted than romantic.

"What happened?" I ask. "Robert's man said I was drugged."

From my hazy memories, I can't recall how something like that would occur. One moment, I was watching him from the doorway, and the next…

"All I know is you were gone and we were being shot at from the woods," Mischa says. "Luckily, Vanya had already moved out with the rest of the men, and I could catch up well enough. Sergei suggested he mount a rescue, but I went out on my own."

Which may explain why the leader looked more irritated than relieved when he arrived, his prize in tow.

"I didn't know where he kept you, though Sergei had a vague idea of the direction they went in," he admits. "Still, I expected to spend days tracking you down. But then…" He chuckles deep in his throat. "I find that you're already ten steps ahead."

"So what happens now?"

"Now?" He eases away from me, but his fingers slide along my hips, dragging out the contact until the last possible second.

When our gazes reconnect, I see a hint of that raw openness from before. But where, when Anna was mentioned, he looked softer—now, his bared teeth portray only ruthlessness.

"I'm going to destroy the Winthorps from the inside out."

"But why not just..." I trail off and let myself envision a fantasy world. One in which I could run away and no evil men would ever follow. I could live my life in peace, doing the things I've only ever dreamt of.

Find a home.

Make it my own.

Start a family...

But even in that beautiful fantasy, one fact cuts through everything like a thorn.

Robert would never let me go.

Maybe Mischa and Sergei are right in their own twisted way. There is only one method to ever fully eradicate the threat from the Winthorps.

Once and for all.

"Don't look so disappointed." Mischa swipes his finger along my chin. "I'll save your chosen prey for last. You can drive the spike through his neck."

I cringe at the imagery and brush my fingers along my jaw, tracing the remnants of Robert's last assault. "And if I don't want to?"

Am I talking to Mischa or myself?

"You want to," he replies regardless. "Oh yes. You fucking want to."

I turn away and head for the door. "We should talk to Vanya… Anna. Maybe she knows something about what Robert is planning."

Deep down, I know she doesn't. On her face, I saw the same doe-eyed expression I assume Mischa did the day he captured me. The stark, naked terror of a bird freshly freed from her cage.

Regardless, he says nothing, though I sense him behind me.

Vanya and Anna are still in the small sitting room. They're sitting as close together as they can, their hands clasped, their foreheads meeting. The boy is asleep on Anna's lap. When she spots me, she stiffens and her arms go protectively around him.

"Ellen," she says, her voice hoarse. "Is that your name? Ellen?" She looks to Vanya for clarification and he nods. "I want to thank you for—"

"Don't," I say thickly. "You don't have to."

"But I must." Sighing, she turns to Mischa. "I can't believe… I can't believe I'm really here—"

"Where did they keep you all this time?" he asks, his tone awkwardly gentle, as if he can't remember quite how to sound comforting. There's a hesitance in him he's never displayed, not even around Mouse. "They told us you were dead," he adds. "If I would have known, I would have done everything I could to—"

"I know." Anna eyes the child sleeping in her arms and strokes his hair. "They kept me at Winthorp Manor at first. I think so anyway. It's all a blur, those early days."

Her knuckles whiten as she fingers a blond curl and then smooths it carefully into place.

"They beat me at first. I thought they were going to kill me, but one day…" She breaks off as if reliving the memory. Her eyes widen and she removes her trembling hands from the boy and balls them into fists. "The older Winthrop. He came into my cell, and all he said to me was, 'My wife is the only reason you're still alive.'"

"Robert, Sr.?" Mischa asks, sounding to me as if he's miles away. "*His* wife?"

A torrent of blood surges through my ears as everything fades.

And all I see is her face.

"Marnie Winthorp," I say. "Her?"

"Yes." Anna nods. "I guess she made him keep me alive."

I blink rapidly, bringing more of the world into focus. The room. Vanya. Mischa. Both of them are staring at me. Watching me.

"They moved me after that," Anna continues. "I don't know where. It was isolated. They never visited much in those early days, but they didn't hurt me, either."

"One of their outposts?" Vanya asks Mischa.

The other man nods. "Most likely."

"I wasn't beaten or anything worse," Anna reiterates. She stares at nothing and I suspect she's speaking more for her own benefit than anyone else's. "They just kept me in a room alone, for years. So many years…" Tears well in her eyes, but she blinks them back. Her lips part into a breathtaking smile as she stares down on the boy in her arms. "If it weren't for him, I would have gone insane."

"What's his name?" Vanya leans forward and brushes his fingers along the boy's side. His wizened features soften for a brief instant and he looks years younger.

"His name?" Anna's gaze darts in my direction and then quickly flits away. "E-Eli," she says. "His name is Eli. Do you remember, Papa?" She croaks a watery laugh. "I always used to say that I would name my firstborn after—"

"Your grandmother." He smiles. "And a fine name it is."

"You said they didn't touch you." Mischa stands stiffly, staring into a past far beyond this room. "Then who is his father?"

"Mischa!" Vanya lurches to his feet. Anger brims over his face, darkening his eyes. For a brief second, he's transformed and I see an echo of the man Mischa claimed he used to be. "Don't." He shakes his head. "Not now."

"I-I'm tired." Anna stands as well, clutching the boy to her chest. He stirs, grumbling, and she cradles his head. "And I should put him down for his nap."

"I'll go with you." Stern-faced, Vanya stands between Mischa and his daughter like a guard, ushering her into the hall.

When they're out of earshot, I whirl on Mischa.

"Does it matter?" My voice comes out louder than I meant it to—I'm practically shouting. "Who his father is? Does that really matter to you? It's obvious she loves him—"

"That's not why…" He shakes his head as his gaze refocuses on me. "You said he kept you in separate rooms?"

Him. Robert.

"Y-yes. Why?"

"Nothing." He shakes his head and then storms into the hall. "It's nothing."

In a day of reunions, I'm ready when Sergei finally comes for me. Like the darkness descending beyond the windows, he appears in the doorway of the small sitting room long after everyone else has left.

"Ellen. Did you sleep all right?" he asks, crossing the threshold. "Was the room to your liking—"

"I'm not taking your bait," I say, cutting to the chase. "If you want to tell me about my family, or my mother—fine. But I won't beg you to—"

"Understandable." He comes to stand beside me and gestures to one of the vacated chairs. "Shall we sit? Don't worry. I will not mention my *bait*, as you so put it. Whatever you ask, I am more than willing to answer."

I copy him warily, perching myself on the chair Anna occupied. It's still warm.

"How did you know my mother? I've already heard the abridged version from Mischa," I add. "But I want to hear it straight from you."

"Marnie Winthorp…" His eyes darken thoughtfully, and he cocks his head. "Should I say that I raped her? Tortured her? Beat her? I'm sure Mischa has filled your head with all sorts of sordid scenarios—"

"Just tell me the truth," I say tiredly. "I want… No, I *need* to hear it from you."

"Well, I never touched her. We never hurt her. If you don't believe me, you can ask Ivan."

"But you took her from her family," I point out. "From her daughter."

"Yes." He nods, turning his gaze to the window. "There was that. But you can rest assured that Ivan didn't force himself on her if that's what you're afraid of."

Hope forms a painful ball at the base of my throat. It's nearly impossible to speak. "How do you know that?"

He shrugs. "Because he loved her. More than I have ever seen him love anyone short of his own daughter. Even his first wife. While he cared for her, Marnie Winthorp had that man's soul in the palm of her hand."

It's strange, hearing it said so starkly out loud. I try to pair the two people I know: gnarled Vanya with beautiful, innocent Marnie. No matter how I arrange their imaginary specters, I can't see it clearly.

"But he let her go back to Robert Winthorp," I say.

"She was recaptured, yes." Sergei sighs. "You will have to ask him why he didn't rescue her, but do not doubt that he loved her."

"Did…" I swallow hard and force the question out. "Did he know about me?"

"I don't think so," Sergei admits. "But knowing my brother… I don't see him being content to let you grow up in that place."

A part of me wants to take comfort in that. At least until I recall how he was with Anna. Why go after one daughter when he clearly had another? One he raised and loved wholeheartedly.

"So what do you want with me now?" I demand.

Sergei holds out his hands defensively. "Nothing. I merely want you to learn about your family, the Vasilevs. Learn our ways."

I raise an eyebrow. "Even with Anna back?"

"Anna…" It's like he takes his time, mulling over the most polite phrasing possible. "Who knows what the Winthorps did to her. Is it really fair to ask her to helm so much so soon?"

"But I can?"

He doesn't reply. Instead, he settles into his chair and observes the ornate lawn visible beyond the window.

Moonlight ghosts the foreign landscape, making it seem more ethereal than real.

"I want you comfortable here, Ellen," he says after a moment. "I won't ask anything of you for a few days. Explore. Ask questions. Have the run of the entire manor." Grunting, he pulls himself to his feet and heads for the door. "How did you find your room?"

"Fine."

"Good." He meets my gaze with a searching look of his own and then steps into the hall. From it, his voice reaches me. "It was your mother's. I hope to see you at dinner. I've ordered my chef to prepare a banquet. A celebration of sorts, but I will understand if you prefer to have it brought to you instead."

I say nothing, listening to his steps retreat.

ischa finds me in the dark. I sense him before his hand lands on my shoulder, painted silver by moonlight.

"You didn't eat." He tugs his grip, hauling me from the seat. "Come."

I let him guide me down the hall, but I'm surprised when we pass the room I recognize as mine and enter another alarmingly close to it.

At a glance, I know it's his. Only he would rebel against finery and comfort. He's stripped the bed of its fancy sheets, and his clothing lies strewn over the floor. Out of everything, the most alarming detail is the tray of food left steaming on a table in the corner.

Apparently, he hijacked the delivery meant for me and brought it here.

"Eat," he commands, nodding to the food. At the same time, he fishes something from his pocket and props a knee on the edge of the bed frame. With one hand, he balances the object over his thigh while manipulating a cloth in the other.

A few seconds pass before I realize what he's doing: polishing his knife.

Turning my back to him, I approach the table. Up close, I discover that not only did he take my tray, but a second one lies beneath a discarded gray shirt. He's barely touched the plump steak or vegetables on it.

I incline my head in his direction. "You didn't eat, either?"

He looks up and shrugs. "Banquets are not my thing."

Another glaring difference between him and Sergei. The older man seems to relish tradition, while Mischa…

Well, he prefers to stab what doesn't suit his preferences.

Near the table is a lone chair that I drag closer and sit on. I eat slowly to the soundtrack of the methodical motion of Mischa's polishing cloth.

Finally, the sound dies off.

"Sergei," he says as I pick at the remnants of food. "What did the old man say to you now?"

My hand stills, dangling a fork above my half-eaten vegetables. "What makes you think he has?"

He laughs. "Because you look like you've seen a fucking ghost. That's why."

I hear the thud of his boots striking the floor as he approaches me slowly. He savors the way I tense with every inch gained.

"And because… I'm not sure I trust him."

He lets the statement linger and I know he's gauging my reaction.

"Do you?" he asks when I remain silent.

I jump as he places his hand beside my half-eaten plate. "I don't know."

For all intents and purposes, the man seems genuine. But so could Robert Winthorp when he wanted to.

In this twisted game of men and money, I've learned that no one can be accurately judged at face value. Except…maybe Vanya.

"He's a cunning, sly old fox, Little Rose," Mischa insists against my ear. His breath fans my skin, erasing a chill I hadn't felt until now. "Maybe it's a family trait. But you've never asked: Why can Vanya barely stand to be in the same room with him? In fact, why would the man pledge his loyalty to *me* over his own brother? Think."

"Why?" I ask on cue. "Though I suspect you'll tell me anyway."

He chuckles, but there's a manic edge to the sound. This, I suspect, he's been itching to tell me for a long time.

"Do you remember?" he wonders, leaning in so that his lips graze my shoulder. I suck in a breath and curl my hands beneath the table to disguise how they shake. "That stupid boy you think you saw all those years ago? The one who saved your life, believing that you were Briar Winthorp?"

"You," I say hoarsely. "I saw you."

He crept into my room and urged me to hide. In the process, he gave me the mantra that saw me through years of torment. *Breathe.*

"But do you know why we were really there, Sergei and I?" He circles around my position and braces his hands against the table from the opposite end. "Ask."

"Why?"

"Revenge," he says simply. "We weren't aiming to merely whisk Briar away, oh no…"

His eyes darken in a way I've never seen before. It makes him look tired in a sense. A man who's seen a lifetime of horrors and hasn't forgotten a single one.

An ominous thrill runs down my spine as I brace my hands over the table's surface. "What were you going to do?"

His jaw clenches as if to reinforce the grim statement he utters. "We were going to slaughter the girl in her bed, Little Rose. Butcher her into pieces."

I wait for a laugh. A scoff. Anything.

As twisted as he can be, no man could be that cruel.

That evil.

But I wait in vain—he won't spoon-feed me this story.

I have to demand it. "Why?"

"As a warning and a lesson," he replies. "Don't ever fuck with the Vasilevs."

CHAPTER 14

I can't disguise the shock distorting my features. My mouth is open, my eyes wide. Finally, I regain my composure enough to rasp, "That's…evil."

"Yes," Mischa agrees, surprisingly earnest. "And if anyone should have agreed with that plan, it should have been Vanya, right? It was *his* daughter we wanted to rescue—or avenge if we couldn't. He, more than anyone, should have been howling for Winthorp blood. But when he heard what Sergei planned…" He frowns, reliving the past. "He was furious. Livid. I didn't understand why, not then. But he threatened his own brother's life if he touched Briar."

For my mother? My heart feels too battered to consider it, so I bite the thought back.

"You agreed with Sergei?" I ask, assuming the obvious: Two men came to me that night, creeping through the shadows of Briar's room.

"I went with him anyway," Mischa admits. "I thought Ivan

was a stupid fool. Anna should have been his focus. Anna…" He grits his teeth and exhales harshly. "But when I saw her—you—I knew then and there which man I wanted to follow. Vanya may have been a fool, but…" He looks up and my heart pangs at what I find: something elusive but real enough that Vanya pledged his life to nurture it. "I've killed men before—with my bare fucking hands, even. But that was different. I couldn't… Not that."

"And that's why Vanya loves you," I interject. "He loves you like a son because he can see the good in you—"

"Or maybe I'm just a feral dog he wants to keep close." He flexes his fingers against the table's surface as if uncomfortable with that assessment. "Whatever his reasons, he left Sergei after that."

My mind spins, fighting to reconcile this new piece of information with what I know now. If Marnie saved Anna, why not tell Vanya? Could she really be so cruel as to allow his daughter to rot in a Winthorp dungeon alone?

But even so, she *did* save his child in the end.

And Vanya saved hers.

"Why didn't you tell me this before?" I ask, returning my focus to Mischa.

"Because of this." He reaches out, flicking his fingers accusingly along my jaw. "That look. Like you know me. Pity me. Tell me." He leans in close, letting his breath ghost my cheek. "Am I worthy of your pity, Rose?"

My reply comes automatically. "Yes."

He may be a brute and a monster and—at times—a psychopath. But his world shaped him this way. Somehow, someway, it hasn't entirely consumed him. Not yet.

"Wrong answer," he scolds as if it's a mortal offense. "You should be afraid of me, Rose. Deathly afraid. Shall I tell you why?" He boldly sweeps his gaze down to the high neckline of my dress and my skin prickles with answering goosebumps. "Because the things I want to do to you... They aren't very nice."

His hand shakes as he reaches for me again, batting another strand of my hair. In the process, he brushes over the place Robert hit me and I flinch. Instantly, he withdraws and something I'm not expecting flickers across his face. Guilt?

"I'll let you decide when I—"

"Tell me." I risk meeting his gaze when he stays silent and my belly clenches at what I find brimming there. Only the most primal terms in my arsenal can describe it: raw, naked lust. "Those things you want to do..." I reiterate before licking my lower lip. "Was it all just talk?"

"Oh?" He chuckles low in his throat, cocking his head. More than ever, he resembles a snarling wolf ready to pounce.

And in response, I bare my throat.

"I want to rip that hideous dress off you, for one." He casts my frock a glance of disgust. "Then I'll wash you. Count those marks and divots in your skin, make sure every hair is still there, just as I left it..."

My breath catches. "And then?"

"I'll remind you," he says. "How to scream the only man's name you're allowed to say in full. Do you remember it?" His eyes flash as my lips part.

"Mischa..."

The involuntary grunt erupting from his throat spurs me on.

"Mikhailovich...Stepanov."

"Good," he praises thickly. His knuckles whiten as he grips the edge of the table. "But that wasn't quite a scream..."

He rises to his full height and approaches me, skirting the barrier between us.

A million nuances in his posture stick out when they otherwise never would. The jerk of his throat betraying a hard swallow. The alarming gleam in his gaze.

How his muscles ripple, thrumming with ravenous intent.

I shudder in anticipation of his touch even before his hand cups my cheek and forces my head back. He eyes me like this, hunting my expression for something I'm not sure he finds when he draws me up to him and presses his mouth to mine.

The kiss is slower than expected. Like two stray animals reconnecting after an unexpected absence. Has their dynamic changed? They're unsure. Slow, searching touches become grasping exploration until they finally deduce what the other intends.

On his end? Corruption.

All at once, he pulls me from the chair and shoves me toward the bed. Seconds later, my dress is on the floor and he's on top of me, guiding himself between my legs. There is no slow, teasing buildup—just surrender.

And possession.

I wake up in Mischa's bed alone. A new tray waits on the table in the corner, containing breakfast, judging from the smell.

Someone also left a pile of clean clothing at the foot of the bed. A smile tugs at my mouth as I inspect my options: a pair of jeans and a simple shirt.

But it's the color that draws my notice: a hated shade of pink. Maybe Mischa's opinion toward the hue has softened after all.

Once I'm dressed, I pick over the food—porridge, eggs, and toast—and then I slip into the hall, fully intending to take Sergei up on his offer.

But where Mischa mockingly goaded me to explore his own manor once, I suspect that Sergei has a different motive in mind, rather than to toy with me.

Now that I know it's where my mother slept, the emerald room takes on a different atmosphere. Admittedly, the plainness holds none of the intrigue Mischa's mother's red room did, and after twenty-four years, there shouldn't be much left to find.

Still, I swallow hard and push the door open, stepping inside as if for the first time.

Closing my eyes, I try to picture her here. Was the door locked behind her? Did she lie on that bed and pine for Briar?

It's no use. The Marnie I knew can only be conjured in the opulent finery of Winthorp Manor, draped in pearls and expensive clothing. I can't think of her as a captive or otherwise.

Maybe Sergei was lying?

But Anna wasn't. My mother saved her life. Would she go so far for a man she hated?

Thinking of it all makes my head throb, and I reenter the hall, closing the door behind me. I don't go far before commotion draws my attention to a nearby window.

Screaming?

My heart skips as I press my fingers against the glass. Is it another attack?

Thankfully, the reality seems far less nefarious.

A small boy runs across an emerald lawn, shrieking at the top of his lungs. Eli—and it doesn't take long before I spot the source of his peril: a monstrous pursuer giving ruthless chase. Blond hair differentiates them both from the dark green of the lawn. From this distance, they resemble two versions of the same figure: one young, the other battered with age.

Suddenly, the larger of the two lunges, snatching the boy from behind, and they both collapse into a heap on the grass.

Not far from them stands Anna wearing a faint smile of her own. To any casual onlooker, they would appear to be the perfect family enjoying a lazy morning. It's almost scary how well Mischa could fit into that mold when he wants to: caring protector. A father…

Watching them together should soothe the ache in my chest, but the discomfort only grows as I turn away.

Alone, I descend the stairs and eventually find my own way out to the garden through a back hallway.

At the center of a small, paved courtyard, Eli is now sitting near a plot of rose bushes, decapitating them while Mouse crouches in the dirt a few yards away.

"Hello," I croak as they turn to me in unison.

"Hello!" Beaming, Eli wrenches a handful of roses from the bush. He waves them absently, spraying blood-red petals over his once-white clothes. "Are you back from heaven for good?"

"W-what?" A startled laugh escapes my throat, surprising me. "I don't—"

"Eli!" Anna calls to him from paces away. "Come here, please."

He looks at me, his nose wrinkling, before he dutifully races toward his mother, leaving me with Mouse.

For once, the girl acknowledges my presence with more than resolute silence. I think I see her mouth twitch slightly. A smile?

She's holding a stick, digging persistently into the earth at the base of the bushes. The closer I come, her markings resemble something more deliberate. Letters?

DONATELLOVAN

She stiffens, noticing my attention, and strikes her stick through the letters, erasing them. Then she stands and darts to another spot of the garden.

Sighing, I turn away and notice Mischa and Anna nearby. A chill washes over me as I watch them. Her slender frame paired with his bulk creates a striking contrast.

They stand close together, speaking in hushed tones. Mischa reaches out, grasping her arm as his lips move fervently. Whatever he says makes her eyes widen and she shakes her head.

"Please, Mischa. Please don't—" She breaks off, noticing my approach. Her thin lips quiver as she forces a smile, but anyone could see the tears welling in her eyes. "H-hello. Excuse me."

She slips past Mischa and scoops Eli into her arms. "You're so filthy," she scolds him playfully. "Time for a bath?" Bouncing him on her hip, she returns to the house.

"She's protective of him," I say and I watch her go, if only to fill the silence. Though what mother wouldn't be, forced to raise a child among the Winthorps?

Mischa says nothing. He stares after her as well, his jaw tight. Then he shakes his head. "You," he declares, pointing to Mouse.

She startles to attention, smoothing her hands along her simple gray dress.

"You still want to learn?" He reaches into his pocket and withdraws a familiar object: his knife.

A slow, bright smile unfolds over Mouse's features and she races toward him.

"Fix your posture," Mischa snaps. "Stand tall—no! Straighter. Good." Like a drill sergeant, he guides her into the right stance and then carefully molds her fingers around the handle of the blade. "Every time you strike, you mean it," he tells her. "You may think a gun is more dangerous, but a knife is just as lethal, and bleeding to death is more painful than having your brains blown out. Trust me on that."

I find myself watching them as I lean against a willow tree. Overall, Mischa makes for a firm though gentle instructor. He corrects her mistakes but praises her accomplishments.

"Good," he says when she stabs at an imaginary foe. "Very good." He eases the blade from her grasp, sheathes it, and returns it to his pocket. "You pick up fast. Now, go. Let's see if you've gotten any better at hiding. If I can't find you before dinner, I'll pay you double."

She takes off, dashing across the gardens. The second she's gone, Mischa levels his searching stare in my direction.

"Tell me," he taunts, beckoning me closer with a jerk of his chin. "I know something is circling that little brain of yours."

"I'm thinking about her," I admit, going with one of the safer topics consuming my thoughts. "Mouse. I'm wondering where she came from. Did you know that she's twelve?"

"She is?" He glances in the direction the girl took off in. "I could always ask Nicolai if he knows more."

"She drew a name into the dirt," I add. "Donatello Van—"

"Vanici?"

From his tone, I sense a grim mixture of admiration and loathing typical for someone he considers a rival.

"A big player in the Italian mob. But I don't think he has a thing for children."

"Would that bother you if he did?" I ask.

He raises an eyebrow "Maybe. Or maybe I'm lying to avoid picking a fight you seem itching to have? Though it doesn't matter." He steps in close. "Don't get too comfortable. I don't plan to stay here long," he murmurs near my ear. "And when I decide to leave, I want you to be ready."

"You sound like we'd have to escape—"

"In any case," he grunts. "Be ready."

I blink, caught off guard by the honesty in his tone. For once, he lets me inside his head, and as chilling a proposition as it is, a part of me is more than eager to finally peek beneath his mask.

"Sergei is planning something," he adds. "After years of inaction, he's suddenly inserting himself into the fray. Something about it feels off. I don't know why yet, but—"

"Do you think he's dangerous?"

He exhales slowly, thinking it through. "I don't know. But the man is always one step ahead. I used to admire that about him, you know. Most men want to shoot their problems in the fucking face."

Himself included.

"But Sergei? He'll make that 'problem' wind up with a bullet in its brain, all without seeming to lift a finger."

"He knew my mother. But not in the way you think." I hesitate. How much of this can I trust him not to spit at me later, twisted into a mocking taunt?

His eyes give me no answers. I have to trust him.

"He kept her here," I add. "Vanya said… He told me that she wasn't his captive." I watch him carefully to gauge his reaction. Did he know that part of the story?

"Interesting." He observes the grand structure behind me, his gaze narrowed. "This place has been in the Vasilev family for generations. Who knows what Sergei has stashed here."

A sudden thought occurs to me. "Do you think Anna knew her, my mother?"

He shakes his head. "I don't know. Anna…" His lips part and close. Whatever he meant to say, he seems to rethink voicing it. Or not. "What do you think of her son?"

I flinch at the intensity of the question. "Her son?"

It's as if, until now, there was a wall in my head, blocking off any thought of Eli. With one question, Mischa breaks that barrier down.

"He's beautiful," I blurt in a rush. "So beautiful. I don't. I never—" I swallow hard, alarmed to find my eyes are watering. Before I can blink them back, tears fall. "I've never been around someone his age before…"

I'm being ridiculous. Furious, I swipe at my cheeks, smothering every bead of moisture into oblivion. Mischa merely watches me, offering neither judgment nor support.

"What about Anna?" I rasp.

Maybe changing the subject to her is my selfish way of turning the tables?

Or perhaps I just want to compound that aching, lingering pinch in my chest. Only now do I feel spiteful enough to name it. *Jealousy?*

"You loved her, didn't you?"

"I did," he admits gruffly. "I *do*. She's family."

"But as something more?" I'm acting childish now, no better than Eli or Mouse. Even so, I can't resist pushing him further. "Could you see yourself marrying her? Once the war with the Winthorps is over."

He strokes his chin. After a moment, he nods. "Yes. I could marry her."

I don't register cringing from him until he grips my shoulders, dragging me back.

"I could," he cruelly insists against my ear. "We'd have a couple of kids. Live in the fucking country somewhere. It would be perfect, Little Rose—except for one thing…"

My heart throbs as I eye the landscape behind him. If he wants me to respond, I don't.

So he answers for me. "Anna isn't a fucking hellcat."

"Bastard!" I lash out with the flat of my hand and he easily evades the blow.

"She's too sweet," he goads. "I don't think she could ride my cock the way you can—"

"You're disgusting," I spit.

But he's laughing and the sound affects me more than if he truly meant his boast. It's real and lilting, and he doesn't even seem to realize he's doing it: feeling something other than rage.

"Hmm." His tongue traces his lower lip. "I'd much rather see you bear my child. I could give you a few. Would you want that?"

"Never!" I thrust my chin into the air indignantly. "What makes you think I'd ever want your baby?"

"You're right." His face falls, and he lets me go. "Why would you?"

I gape as he pushes past me. By the time I recover from shock, he's already halfway to the house.

"Mischa!" I start after him, forced to run to match his pace. Of all the things to prickle through my nerves now, guilt shouldn't be one of them. "Wait!"

He makes me chase him into the foyer, ignoring me every step of the way.

"Mischa." I pant. "Mischa, wait—"

Suddenly, he stops short before the staircase and extends his hand toward me. *Quiet.*

Beyond him, I finally notice the two other figures already in the foyer, their voices raised.

"Are you insane?" a man demands. His tone radiates so much raw anger that I barely recognize it at first. Only as I follow Mischa's gaze do I realize *Vanya* is the one shouting. "Have you lost your goddamn mind, Sergei?"

"Have you, Ivan?" In chilling contrast, Sergei's tone is eerily level. "I'm doing what must be done to protect our name."

"Our name? Or your pride?"

"Why can't it be both?"

"Something tells me that this is more than a brotherly squabble," Mischa says, stepping forward.

It's clear from his positioning near Vanya just whose side of the argument he favors out of the gate.

"What's going on?"

"Have you told him? Your *leader*?" Vanya demands of Sergei. When the latter says nothing, he scoffs. "Of course not. Sergei has called a council tonight in a bid to reinstate himself as acting head. The Pakhan."

From Mischa's fierce expression, it's clear he doesn't approve of such a plan.

"Is that so?" he murmurs, deadly soft. "On what grounds?"

"On the grounds that you are too reckless to lead," Sergei says—but his gaze cuts in my direction. "Among other reasons. The *mafiya* needs stability if there is to ever be peace—"

"Peace?" Vanya spits on the floor at his feet. "You spout peace but forget the Winthorps—you're starting a fucking war within your own goddamn ranks!"

"Am I?" Sergei shrugs. "Perhaps. Perhaps not."

"In the end, this is just pointless." Vanya throws his hands into the air. "Tell him, Mischa!"

"Ivan has a point," Mischa says. "You may have your sway, Sergei, but I doubt that you could even muster enough support for a leadership change regardless."

"Perhaps." Sergei nods. "In any event, my main intent is beyond a respectful challenge."

"Oh?" Mischa says before Vanya can bite back.

"Yes. I'd like to elect a new head to the table—"

"Of course you would," Vanya interjects. "Have you learned nothing all these years? Or are you still so fond of your dirty tricks? Which fool have you groomed to be your whipped dog now?"

"Someone who has more say in ending this war than anyone," Sergei says, inclining his head.

"Oh? And who is that?" Vanya demands.

"The obvious choice: Ellen Winthorp."

"What?"

All three men turn to me, but Mischa's gaze draws my attention the most. He's guarded again in an instant—closed from me in a way he hasn't been since…

Never. Not even the first day, when he ripped off my blindfold and only saw an enemy.

"Ellen?" Vanya seems torn between laughing in disbelief and shaking his head. "With all due respect, what right does she have to sit at the table?"

"She was married to that family," Mischa says before Sergei can voice his own explanation. "She was married to its fucking head. She can have a say." He turns and mounts the stairs, leaving Vanya staring after him open-mouthed.

"M-Mischa—"

"I won't fight the appointment," Mischa declares over him. From the top of the staircase, he adds, "But don't expect me to roll over, Sergei. You want to play politics. We'll fucking play."

"Mischa…" With one last look at his brother, Vanya follows him, his steps resonating through the manor's very foundation.

Their absence drains the room of anger. Left behind is a mixture of Sergei's quiet observation and my own shock.

"What are you doing?" I demand, advancing on the older man.

His eyes flicker over my face, impossible to read. "I'm giving you a chance to state your case," he says. "Do you want an end to this bloodshed? Mischa may have the council stacked in his favor, but you possess one thing that neither he nor I have."

"And what is that?" I rasp.

He carefully tucks a piece of my hair behind my ear, heedless of how I flinch at his touch. "A voice," he says. "Your words alone have more impact than any political savvy. Remember that. I hope to see you tonight. If you don't mind, I've already taken care to have a dress delivered to your room."

He leaves, disappearing down a corridor at the other end of the hall.

In this moment, in the center of the marble flooring, I feel more like a pawn than ever.

And the game is already in checkmate.

CHAPTER 16

I must spend hours pacing this bare fucking room. Marnie's presence feels realer now more than ever. It's like she's mocking me sweetly from the grave: *What are you doing, my Rose? Do what I did. Give in…*

Stubbornly, I pace until the tapping of my footsteps drowns her out—but I don't catch the sound of the door opening until it's too late. My intruder is already inside, closing the door.

"You need to get ready," Mischa snaps, raking his gaze over my rumpled shirt and jeans. "Damn. Do you even have anything to wear—"

His eyes darken as he approaches the bed and inspects the dress Sergei provided. It's a deep navy with a bold neckline, made of silk. Mischa must approve of it, because he snatches the fabric in his fist and throws it in my direction.

"Put it on."

"Why?" I croak, letting the dress land in a crumpled heap at my feet. "Aren't you bored of having me used as a pawn in your twisted games? I know I am—"

"*Sergei* wants you as a pawn," he agrees. "But as for me… I want to see if you even have the balls to play the game. Lift your arms." He stoops for the gown and gestures for me to undress. "Hurry up. They won't take you seriously looking like some naïve innocent, Rose. I can assure you of that."

"How can I trust you?" Even as I voice the question, I stiffly lift the shirt over my head.

"You don't have to," Mischa counters. He steps in close and tugs on the clasp of my jeans himself. "Use your brain. A man like Sergei wants to manipulate you for his own gain. The only way to outmaneuver him is to outsmart him."

"And what about you?"

I'm naked now, painfully aware of how close he is. His breath bastes the flesh of my throat as he drapes the gown over my head and tugs it into place.

I watch him work, hunting his expression for a hint of conniving intent. "What do you hope to gain?"

He looks away. "Believe it or not, Little Rose, I only want the truth… Now, listen. Sergei will invite you to speak. He'll want you to argue against continuing the war with the Winthorps. But is that what you really want?"

Ending the war. The violence. The bloodshed. "Shouldn't that be what you want?"

"Of course." He looks me over—but whatever he sees makes him hiss through his teeth. "Turn around." When I comply, he positions himself behind me and I stiffen as his fingers sink through my hair, parting it roughly.

"What are you doing?"

"Improvising," he grunts in reply. "To answer your question: Of course that's what I want. But I'm not foolish, Rose. I know that wars rarely end with a handshake and goodwill. Someone tends to wind up with a knife in their back. I would rather this end in a hailstorm of fucking fire than…"

"Than what?" I demand when he falls silent.

"Than in checkmate." He continues to tug at my hair, arranging it with far more confidence than a man like him should have. Once finished, he spins me around and nods in approval. "With Sergei Vasilev at the head of the gameboard, I can't win this round, but you can. And *now*, you're ready."

He guides me into the bathroom and I catch sight of our reflections in the mirror.

"You're good with your hands," I grudgingly admit.

The woman standing before him is a stranger at first. Her hair has been expertly coiled into a knot at the nape of her neck. The navy of her gown highlights the blue of her eyes. For a second, it's like I'm staring into the past at someone else. The only difference is the prominent scar proclaiming my place in this war: fifteen.

"You look the part," Mischa admits.

My opinion differs. "I look like my mother."

"A player," he corrects. From him, such a term might be a compliment. "But now you need to decide what role you will play. And trust and believe, Little Rose—I won't go easy on you this round."

I flick my fingers along the silk skirt of the dress. "What do I need to expect?"

The last *mafiya* gathering I attended proceeded much like an outlaw court.

Where transgressions were paid for in blood.

But this meeting, with power on the line?

My brain shies away from envisioning it.

"Politics," he replies. "I trust Vanya with my life—but he is an optimist. If he truly wanted power, Sergei would already have it. For some reason, he seeks to use you." He brushes my cheek and scowls at his fingers. "Do you remember the man you saw with Nikolaus the night he attacked you?"

I swallow the memories back. "Yes. You brought me to him as well."

"Before I knew he was a fucking traitorous prick," he insists. "But he would have never had the balls to ally against me without sniffing something in the air. Rats are opportunistic, Rose. They only strike when it's to their advantage."

"So what do I do?"

His lips twitch, part grimace, part smile. "Be the daughter of a Vasilev—but never forget what leverage you have in your possession."

With that ominous warning, he steers me back into my room, and together, we enter the hall.

"When we reach the bottom of these stairs, we won't be allies," he warns.

But I marvel at his use of the word. Have we ever been so aligned? His tone didn't sound mocking.

"I didn't ask for this," I point out.

"And that's why you need to fucking fight." He snatches my hand, gripping tight, and I stare at our entwined fingers: his rough and callused, mine slim and pale.

With every step, we draw closer to the line he's drawn—once past it, we're enemies again.

But he takes his time.

And so do I.

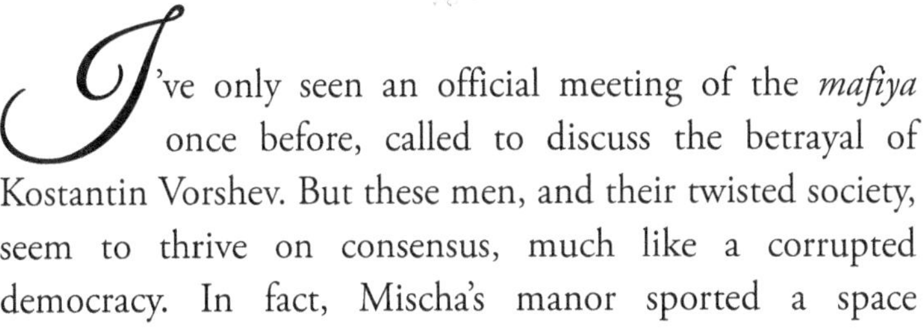

I've only seen an official meeting of the *mafiya* once before, called to discuss the betrayal of Kostantin Vorshev. But these men, and their twisted society, seem to thrive on consensus, much like a corrupted democracy. In fact, Mischa's manor sported a space designed for the sole purpose of hosting an enormous gathering.

Unsurprisingly, Sergei's home contains such a room as well, located at the rear of the house. It's spacious, its layout resembling a great hall. Wood-paneled walls create an enclosed atmosphere as marble flooring magnifies every footstep Mischa and I take over it.

In a grim bit of irony, I recall the pomp and circumstance that took place at Winthorp manor whenever a gathering was hosted there. Such an event would require months of preparation and organization—and if so much as a napkin color deviated from expectation, it would be deemed a massive failure.

In contrast, Mischa and his ilk seem to thrive on converging with barely an hour's notice.

Already, the room is partially filled with men and women gathered around a circle of eleven chairs positioned at the heart of the space. The impromptu layout evokes a sense of authority nonetheless. Those without power to their name seem to congregate on the outskirts, leaving a generous swath of space beyond the seating.

There doesn't appear to be a general consensus as to the dress code of this occasion. Some of the onlookers sport suits or dresses like mine. Others wear leather and jeans.

Dressed in his fatigues, Mischa approaches a chair slightly taller than the others, ornately carved. Meeting my gaze, he nods to one a few seats down. Warily, I approach the chair and perch myself on it.

Not long after, Sergei and Vanya arrive. The elder brother takes a seat across from Mischa, while Vanya stands beside his leader. As the room fills to capacity, Sergei rises, drawing all eyes to him.

Unlike Mischa, he opted for a black suit, expertly tailored to cast a subtle air of intimidation. He wouldn't belong at a Winthorp gathering—that's for sure.

"I've called a council for one reason only," he says, his voice booming to the farthest reaches of the room without the need for a microphone. "To put an end to this war. Mischa, while he may lead us bravely, will have us continue down a never-ending path of violence. Fortunately, I see another way to end this conflict."

"And how is that?" someone demands from the crowd.

"It's simple: We come to an arrangement with the younger Winthorp. Rumor has it that he is shrewder than his father ever was."

"Rumor?" Mischa scoffs. "Rumor has it that I dine on children for breakfast and bathe in their blood. Fortunately, at least *one* of those isn't true."

Uneasy laughter rumbles from those gathered, but the tension is palpable in the air. It's as if invisible battle lines have been drawn, apparent in the subtle body posture of those seated at the circle. Some eye Mischa intently, attuned to his every word. Others look to Sergei.

"The point is: I believe we should end this war now," Sergei insists.

"But we've taken a vote before," another man points out. "I doubt hearts have changed so quickly."

"Really?" Sergei glances at me and moves to stand in the center of the circle. "Then perhaps you'll listen to a voice other than mine? Ellen, would you join me?"

I swallow hard, choking a refusal down. My trembling legs barely seem capable of supporting my weight. As all eyes turn to me, it's a wonder I don't melt into a puddle.

One gaze burns more intensely than the others, however. He doesn't take his eyes off me for a second, even as Sergei stands aside, leaving me in the center of the circle alone.

My surroundings blur as what seems like a hundred faceless people focus on me.

"And who is this?" someone asks.

"She is Robert Winthorp's wife," Sergei says, receiving startled gasps. "I believe it is only fair that she should have a say in this conflict."

More murmurs rise from those gathered. "And what does she have to say?"

"Before we begin, *I'd* like to make a suggestion," Mischa cuts in. He sits casually in his chair, his arms crossed, but his eyes are fiercely alert. "As someone pointed out, we've already settled this matter via a vote. But as Pakhan, I'm willing to let her decision overrule any previous course of action. All opposed?"

A smattering of people dissent, but presumably not enough to make a difference.

"Then it's settled," Mischa says. He and Sergei share a searching look, but the other man makes no objection. "In fact," Mischa continues, "I say we go a step further: We give her a seat at the table with all the authority of an acting head."

"Are you serious?" someone scoffs.

"No."

"Out of the question!"

"Oh?" A flicker of emotion distorts Sergei's otherwise cold expression. Curiosity? "On what grounds would you make such a suggestion?" he wonders.

"It's simple." Mischa stands, and even the novelty of my appearance is no match as he effortlessly commands the attention of the entire room. "Not only is she the daughter of Robert Winthorp Senior's first wife, but she's also the bastard of Ivan Vasilev."

Chaos. A chorus of shouting nearly drowns out Mischa's calm, persistent baritone.

"Not only that. But she's the mother of Robert the younger's sole surviving heir."

I can't breathe. No matter how rapidly I suck air in, none of it seems to go into my lungs. It's ironic in a sense: Nikolaus broke my ribs. But Mischa shatters the pathetic organ trapped between them. Blood pools in my veins, stalled by an ineffective heart.

Though he did warn me: *When we reach the bottom of these stairs, we won't be allies...*

"Enough!" Someone grabs my arm, radiating gentleness. Vanya. "Mischa, what is the meaning of this?"

Either Mischa doesn't hear him or he ignores him.

"Silence!" The Pakhan raises his hand, radiating authority. "I have proof of my accusations, of course," he says once the clamor fades to a disturbed hum. His eyes scan the crowd and then land on one figure. Alarmingly, his gaze softens and my throat tightens even before he calls them by name. "Anna..."

A hush falls over the room as all eyes turn to the pale woman practically huddled in a corner. Shaking, she starts forward, tears streaming down her cheeks.

"Mischa, please," she gasps in between sobs. "Mischa, *please—*"

"Anna." His expression hardens. "Tell them. No harm will come to him, but you need to tell them. Now."

Trembling at the edge of the circle, Anna looks smaller than ever. A shadow of a woman, likely to fade into the ether with one wrong move. Vanya's grip tightens on my arm, but for whatever reason, he doesn't go to her.

"I…" She swallows hard and clears her throat. "I am Anna-Natalia Vasilev—"

"And for sixteen years, she was a prisoner of the Winthorps," Mischa finishes for her. "They kept her locked in a virtual cage while sending a stranger's body to her father. And what else did they make you do?"

More tears streak the woman's beautiful face and she staggers. One of the men near her lurches to his feet and lowers her onto his vacated chair.

"Four years ago, the younger Robert Winthorp brought me…"

"What," Mischa prods. "It's all right."

"He brought me a baby," she admits, her body heaving. "A newborn. He told me to raise him. There were other nannies throughout the years, but I've been with him the longest. I was told that his mother was dead. But when he got older, the story changed…"

"How?" Mischa crosses over to her and places his hand on her shoulder. "Tell them."

"He… He told him she was an angel, and that—one day, if he was good enough—he might bring her to see him."

It's a lie. It has to be a lie—no man could be that cruel. No woman could be *that* naïve. But horror renders me paralyzed regardless. I can clearly picture Robert performing every action described.

And it guts me to my core.

"A few months ago, he gave him a locket," she says hoarsely. "He said it contained his mother's picture." She looks at me. "*Her* picture."

"Is this the locket?" Mischa reaches into his pocket and withdraws a golden chain. From it dangles a square-shaped charm. God, I recognize it…

The chain I saw around Eli's neck.

"Yes." Anna hunches over herself, clutching her chest. "Y-yes."

The room descends into roars not even Mischa can overrule. A sea of voices and noise and grasping hands. I lash out, shoving my way through until I'm free of the press of people. Then I run until my shaking legs deposit me on the floor of a distant room and I'm alone.

But not for long. My pursuer betrays himself before he even finds my hiding place.

"Get up, Rose."

"Maybe this truly is just a game to you," I rasp, looking up and finding him in the doorway. "But this is my life!"

"A life you've been hiding from," he points out.

"How could you do that to Anna?"

"Anna?" He sounds harsher than I've ever heard him. "Don't fucking lie to me. You knew. You knew that child was yours the second you saw him. But you were afraid. Afraid to face the pain, and the anger, and the rage. I can understand that. But the time has come, Rose. You can't escape the truth forever."

"Truth?" I spit. "As if you give a damn about me. Admit it! All you wanted was to outwit Sergei and humiliate me!"

He blinks, and beneath the anger and rage, a suspicion gnaws away at the back of my mind: Maybe, for one brief second, the man feels some semblance of guilt.

But it's still not enough.

"I hate you for this," I spit, my voice breaking. "God, I hate you—"

"No, you don't," Mischa says. "You hate him. He manipulated and abused and lied to you for sixteen years. He turned your pain into a weapon, but now, you have the chance to do something about it. End the feud, or decide to run him into the ground. The choice is yours to make." He starts through the doorway, but near the threshold, he pauses. "But know this… Whatever you choose, I'll stand by it. If only to see you break the mold of a fucking pawn and finally play the game."

He leaves, and in his absence, I haul myself to my feet, using the wall as a crutch. My mind reels, and a million conflicting emotions wrestle for control of my heart. Too many to decipher all at once. I can't. My only course of action in this moment is to dry my tears and retrace my steps.

With effortless authority, Mischa and Sergei have regained control of the room, but the battle lines are even more defined. A virtual barrier splits the room in half. There is no question now as to who belongs to what side, save for two lone figures lingering on the outskirts of the hall.

One is Vanya, staring far away into the distance. Clinging to him is Anna. She looks at me, her eyes reddened and bloodshot, and quickly turns away, burying her face against her father's shoulder. He strokes her absently, and with every pass of his hand through her hair, the fractures in my soul deepen.

"Have you made your decision?" Sergei wonders from the circle.

"Yes," I croak. "But first… I need to say something." My gaze travels to Mischa and he stiffens, wary. "I've only ever known the Winthorps," I admit to the crowd, my voice growing in strength. "I was born in the manor, and for nearly twenty-four years, it was my prison…"

The hall remains silent as I finish my tale. It's almost funny how briefly my story can be summed up—barely a few minutes, I suspect. Yet every word has scraped the inside of my throat raw. I can barely suppress the horrors I've fought years to push back. They're conjured by my boldness in addressing them.

But in a sense, I feel lighter from having finally voiced them.

"I, more than anyone, should want to fight Robert Winthorp with every fiber of my being out of spite and revenge," I admit. "But that is not why I'm deciding how I am. It's because I know, deep in my soul, this will never end any other way."

"And your choice?" Sergei demands, his tone decidedly colder.

Mischa is watching me as well. Like always, it's nearly impossible to decipher him.

"I vote to continue the war," I say. "But not for myself, or Mischa, or any other argument."

I merely know the truth: There is no such thing as peace.

"Then it's decided," Mischa says, but I can't ignore the added harshness to his tone.

Neither he nor Sergei is pleased with my decision, it seems. Though admittedly for different reasons.

Sergei lost this round.

But Mischa seems unwilling to accept a victory.

"Council adjured."

Very few members disperse. Most crowd the center of the room, battling for an audience with Mischa or Sergei. I've only caused more chaos, but I don't stick around to see it unfold.

I push my way through the crowd and escape, racing down the hall, up the staircase, and into the barren room unofficially designated as mine.

Here, in the dark, I strip my dress and crawl beneath the bedsheets. The silence feels mocking after the deafening noise in the council chamber. My breathing scratches unevenly at the quiet—a fitting soundtrack for the creak of my doorknob being tested a second later.

"Please don't come to gloat," I plead into my pillow. "Please…"

Soft footsteps inch closer toward my bed despite the warning. They're far too soft to belong to a man, Mischa or otherwise.

"Mouse?" I lift my head and spot her slight shadow along the wall. "Are you here for Mischa?"

Unsurprisingly, I'm not given an answer. The mattress shifts as a lighter body climbs onto the end. Resolutely, they sit while I sob, offering no comfort or judgment.

Nothing at all.

I know that this conversation must happen, even before I wake up to an empty room and don my simple blue dress. Vanya is already lurking in the hallway near my door, his graying hair gleaming silver in the shadow.

When he sees me, he sighs and inclines his head for me to follow. Were I bold enough to claim a resemblance between us, it might be in our actions more than anything. We both dread the inevitable.

Vanya's chosen battleground is the small sitting room overlooking the gardens. Rather than claim one of the leather chairs, he leans against the wall.

"Your mother," he begins gruffly, "because I do not doubt that she was your mother…" Looking at me seems to hurt him. He turns away, raking his fingers through his hair.

"But I don't know what lies you were told. Or by whom. But I don't—"

"She never told me," I admit hoarsely. "Not about my father. I asked her about his identity once and…I was never brave enough to ask again."

"No," Vanya insists. I hear him swallow as if fighting to form words. "I can't be… She wouldn't do that—no." His eyes flash as they rake me over. From Marnie's blue eyes, to my brown hair, to my bare, battered feet. "She wouldn't keep something like that from me. Never. She wouldn't do that to me!"

Tears spill down my cheeks. "I'm sorry. I don't know how to prove it to you. I'm not sure if I even believe it myself…"

Of all the things to cross my mind, something Sergei said during one of our first meetings slithers across my thoughts. A name, uttered like a ghost's.

"Does the name Elena mean anything to you?"

"It was my mother's," he says absently. "She knew… My first wife demanded we name Anna after her mother and grandmother. I always boasted that my next child would be named after mine."

And maybe Marnie was more cunning in her deception than even Robert Winthorp knew. She named me Ellen, a subtle take on Elena—the name she only dared to call me on my birthday.

Along with another moniker.

"You called her Rose, didn't you?" I ask.

His face falls and I almost regret mentioning it in the first place. "Yes. I called her Rose. They were her favorite—"

"You gave her the necklace, too," I surmise. "The one Sergei gave to me. I know you've seen it."

"I have," he admits. "But it wasn't his to give. I never knew she left it behind…"

I can tell through his tone alone that he would have never retrieved it himself.

"I guess she enjoyed manipulating us both," I say.

Vanya looks at me sharply and steps away from the wall. With one hand, he parts my hair and cups my cheek. Then he wraps his arms around me, pulling me close.

"I knew from the moment I saw you who your mother was," he confesses to my shock. "I thought maybe she took another man under the nose of her husband."

Yet he still treated me with nothing but kindness.

"I would have deserved it. I let her go," he continues. "It damn near killed me, but when she left, I let her go. But if I had known… I would have never abandoned you. Never."

I don't doubt him, and deep in my soul, I know that Marnie didn't, either.

She knew a man like him would never throw his child to the wolves.

So she stayed silent.

But something in his tone sticks out, unwilling to fit in the puzzle Sergei and Mischa have forced me to put together.

"Left?" I pull back enough to meet his gaze. Instantly, I know he won't lie to me. Not now. "You make it sound like she had a choice."

In my own case, I didn't choose to return to Robert—and Mischa, for all his twisted jealousy, had been willing to come after me.

"Why did you leave her there?"

"You don't understand," Vanya says. He lets me go and moves to the window, bracing his hands over the glass. With his head bowed, it's easier than ever to see the pain—both emotional and physical—his body has endured throughout the years. "Marnie Winthorp wasn't taken, or kidnapped, or whatever story you've been told. She *chose* to leave her husband—"

"What are you saying?"

"The truth." He scoffs. "We didn't ransom her. She allied herself with Sergei. And with me."

Nothing in all of my twisted journey since being taken has affected me with the same hopeless sense of disorientation. Not Mischa. Or Nikolaus' attack. Or even the cruel reality that Robert may still be alive.

"She grew fearful of her husband. She wanted safety for her and her daughter. When she left, she tried to bring her as well, Briar, but something went wrong and the girl was left behind. Sergei perpetuated the rumor to protect her. In a way, I think he thought it served him as well, the image of a ruthless foe against the greedy Winthorp. But Marnie… All she wanted was a better life. A simple life."

"And you trusted her?"

He nods. "She gave us more than enough information to prove her intentions. She was smart, so smart. And so cunning. She could inspire a fish to live on land just by telling him to. Last night at the council…" He sighs wistfully. "You looked so much like her."

I try to reconcile this brave, bold woman with the fearful specter I knew who could show me affection only in secret.

I can't.

"She was an amazing woman," Vanya insists as if reading my mind. "Don't you doubt that for a second. She was."

"Then why did she leave you? If she was so afraid of her husband and so determined to live a better life, then why go back?"

He flinches. "Your sister. Every day without her pained her a little more. I knew that. And maybe I cared for her more than she did me. I could live with that. I *have* lived with that. But…" He looks at me and his gaze hardens. "She knew how to reach me, and if she so much as hinted about you—" He breaks off, grinding his teeth. "No Winthorp stronghold would have kept me out. She knew that. I loved that woman," he admits. "At least the woman I thought she was."

And maybe, in her own way, she cared for him.

"My name," I say. "I think she wanted it to be Elena."

He winces, gritting his teeth.

"I spent so long being afraid of who my father might be. But I never dreamed that he could be someone like you."

His mouth lifts into the semblance of a smile. "I am sorry you grew up in the way that you did," he says. "But I am proud to finally meet the woman you are."

I approach him, and he doesn't resist the hand I tentatively place on his shoulder.

"But there is still one thing I don't understand," I confess. "You say she wasn't your captive, but Sergei and Mischa seem to believe that she was."

"Mischa?" He cocks his head thoughtfully. "He doesn't know. I've never told him the truth. With Marnie gone, it was easier to maintain the lie. But Sergei?" His body goes rigid. "Sergei can be the staunchest ally you have ever had on your side. And he can also be more ruthless than every single Winthorp combined. I have never doubted his intentions, but you should always question his methods."

"Is that why you decided to support Mischa instead?"

"There came a time when Sergei crossed the line," he says. "He proposed a plan so despicable that I gave him only one option: step down or I would challenge him. So he did."

"He wanted to hurt Briar," I say. Butcher her, as Mischa put it.

"I should have gone with them," Vanya says. "Not only to stop them, but… Perhaps I could have stopped her."

My mother. Not long after that night, she did the unthinkable.

"But it's in the past," he says, pulling away. "There's no use in dwelling on it. All I can do is prepare for the future, and I will not make the same mistake again." He reaches out, ghosting his fingers along my cheek. Then he abruptly turns, limping for the door. "We will talk more later," he promises. "Later…"

I watch him go, unsure of what remains to be said.

Or perhaps it's painfully obvious: We both spent years seeing Marnie Winthorp as merely a victim.

When, all along…she may have been the villain.

CHAPTER 18

My head throbs in the aftermath of Vanya's confession. Desperate for fresh air, I retreat to the gardens.

But all I find are shadows of the past.

Grim, overcast daylight paints the landscape in a silvery glow and I'm reminded of my comfortable prison in Winthorp Manor.

Was this how Marnie felt once freed from her own cage?

Overwhelmed. Exhausted. Terrified.

Rather than learn how to brave this new, dangerous world, she preferred the one she already knew and a more familiar monster.

But I always endured Robert. Understanding him beyond his surface brutality was a chilling prospect. He corrupted everything he touched, myself included. But as a childish bit of laughter reaches my ears, I'm forced to wonder just how far his taint has truly spread.

Up ahead, Eli runs across a patch of grass, his blond curls bouncing wildly. A watchful Anna hovers nearby. She calls to him and he giggles back, so oblivious to the darkness swirling around him through no fault of his own.

Darkness one man conjured purely out of selfish spite. I know he's behind me, even before his hand brushes my shoulder.

"We need to talk—"

"You put a target on his head." Fury distorts my voice. I doubt he can even understand me. "Even if he is—no. It doesn't matter. You've just made him the top prey of any sick bastard who thinks that he can use Robert Winthorp's son as a bargaining chip. Was humiliating me truly worth so much?"

"No one will touch him," he swears, and despite everything, I believe he thinks that. "And as for Sergei? You think *he* is the reason I'd hand the wife of my enemy a seat at the fucking table?"

The harshness in his tone makes me remember the role he and Sergei elected me to: a head.

"What does it even mean?" I demand as he comes to stand beside me.

"You have that power you crave, Rose," he coldly replies. "Enough to do way more than pout in the shadows if you wanted to. Not only that, but do you think I'd announce before the whole fucking world that I have access to not one, but two people Robert Winthorp would kill to reclaim? Leverage I have yet to use. Don't think it hasn't crossed my mind." He laughs darkly, revealing that it has. Multiple times. "But no. I didn't do it for him. I did it for *you*."

"Me?" I scour the tightness of his jaw, searching for any nuance in his expression.

Downcast, his gaze reveals nothing.

"He has your eyes." His voice is so gruff that I barely hear him. His own eyes track the boy as he races around a bed of flowers. "And that bastard…he told him about you, did you know that? He taunted him with your picture. Told him you were dead. Though I'll admit it: I knew even before I saw him that he was still alive."

I stare at my hands, envisioning the life ripped from them four years ago. In such a relatively short time, he's grown into his own person. All without me.

Only someone like Mischa could clearly *anticipate* such a reality.

"How?"

"Because I know how Winthorp's sick, twisted brain works —that's how. He may have resented your pregnancy, but there's no way in hell he would deny himself of not one, but *two* people he could manipulate and control to worship only him. And to ensure as much, he'd keep you apart and use your own longing for each other as a prison. That is the kind of man he is."

He sounds far too confident in that assessment. In the pit of my soul, I know why: In another world, he might have done the same thing. The truly evil Mischa who would have killed Briar without hesitation and whom even Vanya couldn't save.

"And if Eli is my son?" I demand. "What will you do now? Lock him away if I don't support your stupid war? Threaten to sell him? No—" My heart won't let me even consider it. "I'll kill you if you do. I swear I will—"

"What I want?" He pulls ahead too quickly for me to keep pace. Like a storm cloud, he descends on the idyllic scene, heading right for the boy.

"M-Mischa." Anna pales when she sees him. "Eli," she calls, but the boy doesn't seem to hear her.

"It's all right." Once he reaches her, Mischa places his hand on her back. "It's all right."

She looks at me warily as Mischa tries to lead her down a path. Her gaze cuts to Eli.

"It will be all right," Mischa says.

They don't go far. Just far enough that Eli turns, confused to find me instead. His eyes cautiously meet mine, but he doesn't say a word. He merely continues to play, chasing specters in between the rose bushes. Cackling, he decapitates a bloom at random, scattering the petals at his feet like so many droplets of blood.

There is something so beautiful in his innocence.

So painful.

Tendrils of hope and fear encircle my heart, piercing and encasing it. Like vines studded in thorns.

My mother said that hell was like a rose—but that was the nicest way of phrasing it.

War, violence, and death can cause untold pain, but one emotion above all delivers the truest form of agony.

It slices you into pieces, but you can't help but relish every gaping, bleeding wound.

I once told Mischa I'd never felt love.

But that was a lie.

I've never stopped feeling it.

And now?

All I can do is watch its original source, oblivious to the passage of time.

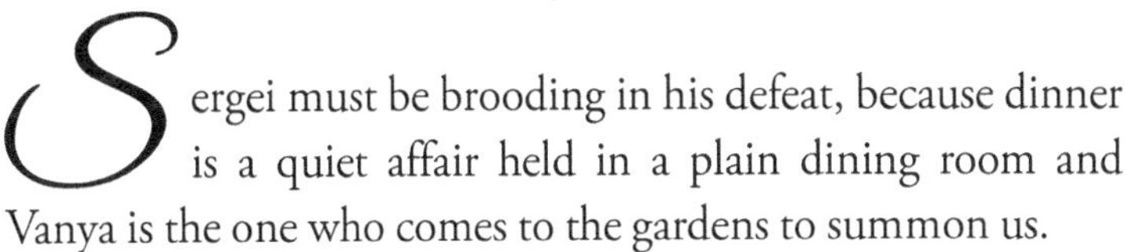

Sergei must be brooding in his defeat, because dinner is a quiet affair held in a plain dining room and Vanya is the one who comes to the gardens to summon us.

Eli skips to Anna, who bundles him in her arms, while Mischa lurks at the outskirts of our ensemble, watching me.

He doesn't stay long. After downing a glass of wine and a few bites of food, he stands and declares, "I'm going to train." On his way through the doorway, he points to Mouse and then Eli. "You two. Come and learn."

Both children scramble toward him in a stampede.

Anna starts to stand as well. "I don't think that's a good—"

"Eat," Mischa says. He grabs Eli and throws the boy onto his back while Mouse slinks past him, darting into the hall. "We won't be long."

Vanya stands as well. "I'll make sure no one loses an eye," he mumbles on his way out.

Finally, Anna sighs and meets my gaze. "I don't want you to think that I'm some evil, selfish woman—"

"I don't."

She inhales sharply and stares down at her hands. "He... He's all I have. I've spent four years devoting every waking moment to him. And now..." Her eyes meet mine accusingly. "You're a stranger. How can I just abandon him? I'm the only mother he's ever known."

I say nothing.

"I knew you weren't dead," she says after a moment. "Even though Robert insisted. I knew. I just thought you were some rich, careless woman who didn't want him. Maybe thinking as much made it easier to hate you. I couldn't feel sympathy for that woman. It *did* make it easier. I could give him everything if his mother never wanted him in the first place."

"I don't expect you to stop loving him," I rasp, my throat tight. "I don't—"

"You just want to know him," she says. "Deep down, I know that. But I can't help feeling like…" She chokes a sob back and tears at her hair. "Like I've woken from a nightmare, but everything I've ever had now belongs to someone else. Honestly, I'm not sure if I prefer the nightmare."

She's referring to more than just Eli. Vanya? And Mischa.

"I don't think I can ever stop seeing him as my son."

"You don't have to," I say in a rush. "But I want… I want to learn to see him in that way too."

Marnie hid me from the world. Maybe she was ashamed of who my father was. But I know now that I refuse to do the same. There is no mistaking that Eli has parts of Robert.

But, as Mischa pointed out, he also contains pieces of me.

"I don't want to take him from you," I admit to Anna. "I couldn't."

"And it isn't my place to deny him his mother," she replies, smiling weakly. "Even if I wish he could stay mine forever."

In awkward silence, we pick at our food. Finally, Anna reaches across the table, brushing her hand over mine. "You aren't hungry?"

I look down at my untouched plate. "I don't think so," I say.

"I see…" She eyes me for so long that I'm not sure whether to question her or leave. Finally, she sighs. "Robert wasn't a terrible father, per se. In fact, I don't think he even knew how to be one. He kept his son well-fed and protected, but he never held him. He never soothed him when he cried. He saw him rarely… Mischa?" Her gaze turns wistful and darts toward my stomach. "Misha would be different. Anyway, I think I'm going up to bed."

She gingerly gathers up her plate and I copy her. Together, we ascend the stairs, silent creatures, victims in this brutal war.

We've both lost an untold amount as collateral.

But in a twisted way, we've gained more than we could ever have imagined as well.

CHAPTER 19

Of all the places in the world, a cold, foreboding fortress should be the last one would expect to find children shrieking through the winding corridors, chased by a specter whom I can only discern from their giggles is the worst kind of monster.

The kind whose identity is alarmingly easy to suspect as I rise from my bed and get dressed in a pair of jeans and a loose-fitting top.

I leave my room only to be nearly run over by Mouse. Grinning, she skirts past me and rounds a corner. Not far behind is Eli, cackling madly. Bringing up the rear is a stranger. A care-free laugh booms from his chest as he moves slowly, ensuring that every footstep echoes like thunder.

"I can hear you," he growls as the children scatter deeper into the house. "You better run—"

His wicked grin falls flat the moment he spots me, and the illusion is shattered.

"Rose." Drawing himself to his full height, Mischa inclines his head toward my room, a subtle command. *We need to talk.*

After everything he's put me through, I should run. I start to, but he's beside me in a second. His fingers interlace with mine, locking tight when I try to wrench away. He all but shoves me into my room before quietly closing the door.

"As much as you love to play the victim, I won't let you this time," he warns. "You can hate me if you want. But don't you dare skulk around like a fucking prisoner—"

"Then how should I act after having my personal drama exposed to your fucking society?" I ask, jutting my chin into the air. "You tell me."

He chuckles under his breath. "Like this," he admits. I shudder as he brushes his hand down my shoulder. I was on guard for violence—not this. "A haughty little bitch. One who may have a point—"

"A point? Maybe I should lead by example?" I suggest, shrugging him off. "I'll share my own little secret in private, without an audience."

"Oh?" He cocks his head as his expression darkens. "Let me guess: Robert Winthorp still has your soul and it was never really mine to claim? A bit anticlimactic, Rose, but not entirely unexpected—"

"No." Balling my hands into fists is the only way I can keep from hitting him. "I… I think I'm pregnant."

He blinks and that mask he wears so doggedly around me cracks. "Are you sure?" His gaze lowers to my stomach. "Is it mine?"

I slap him—but his question didn't trigger the action. It's how he asked it. Hesitant and coarse, as if he wasn't sure of the answer.

And, for once, his confusion isn't played as a joke.

"Who else's would it be?"

He frowns and I understand.

"Fine." I throw my hands into the air, forcing a cold laugh. "It's Robert's. I threw myself at him after being dragged back into my old cage. Does that make you feel better? Now, you have three pieces of 'leverage' to use against him—"

"Stop it." He grabs my arm, but the touch lacks any malice. He merely uses the limb as a leash, keeping me close. "Tell me."

"Does it matter to you so much?" I demand, exasperated.

"Maybe I just need to hear you say it?" His voice deepens, radiating a warning. "Is it mine?"

"Forget it." I shake my head and laugh again. I sound insane. Maybe I am. He's finally driven me past the brink.

"Forget all of it. It's not like someone like you could ever be a father anyway."

He recoils. "And what kind of woman would willfully deny her child one?" His voice chases me as I lunge for the door and throw it open. "A selfish bitch, though why am I surprised?"

"Don't," I whisper hoarsely as my steps falter in the doorway. "Don't you dare."

I brush my hand against my chest, a weak protection against an impending assault.

Like any wolf, he doesn't just bite.

He aims to maim.

"It's in your blood," he hisses. "Like mother like daughter."

I run, racing past a corner where giggles emanate. Panting, I leave the house and venture beyond the outskirts of the woods, vanishing beneath the trees.

Sergei Vasilev owns miles of land. I walk until my legs ache and I can't go a step farther, but I have yet to approach a barrier or land marker. For all of Mischa's hatred of the Winthorps, what makes his world any different? The secrets are the same, as are the twisted lies. Which man's story is more accurate. Sergei's? Or Vanya's?

Hunched against the trunk of a tree, I can't decide. My heart warns me to trust one man more than the other. Vanya. But that muscle is a fickle fucking thing. It hurts now when I think of Mischa, but not in the way that it should. I need to hate him. Despise him. Anything but parse over the agony I saw lurking in his expression.

Like I was the one who hurt him despite the man doubting me at every turn.

But so what if he does? It's growing increasingly apparent that everyone in my life has only ever seen me as a tool, or a burden, or a secret to hide. Never as a living, breathing, bleeding person with a soul of her own.

I should just run. Disappear into the ether and leave the war and its casualties behind. My heart pangs as I think of Eli, but he already has a mother. Yes. I shift to my knees and feel along the tree bark for a branch to help me stand.

I find one, but it breaks off the second I apply pressure and falls onto my shoulder, lashing at my cheek. Laughing, I ignore the slight pain and curl into a ball.

I could fade here instead. Just let the world go on without me.

As if it would be that easy.

I hear them first: footsteps crashing through the undergrowth. Then his voice rings out, more grated than ever.

"Fuck… No, fuck!"

I open my eyes as he staggers toward me and snatches the branch away.

Frantic, he grabs my shoulders. "Can you hear me? Rose? Can you hear me?" He brushes the hair back from my face and sways when he sees me staring back.

"I'm fine," I admit.

"Thank God." He stands, helping me to my feet.

"I'm going back if that's what you're worried about," I say, starting in the direction I assume the manor is in. "I don't require an escort—"

"Fine. So it's Robert's." He grabs me from behind, sliding his hands to my waist. "You can even name it after him. I don't care."

The heat in his voice eats away at any anger I feel. All that's left is just…pain.

"Don't you ever doubt me like that," I say hoarsely. "Never."

"I won't," he swears into the skin of my throat. "I won't… But you don't leave."

I blink rapidly and swallow, fighting for air. "I want to trust you, but every time I try… You attack me."

"Something in me won't let me believe you, Rose," he admits. "Even if I want to. I can't. If I let you in, you'll hollow me out. You'll rob me of everything I have left, and I need to fucking fight. Or I'll be like—"

"Vanya?" I ask.

His arms tighten, giving me his answer. "He told me a story once," he says gruffly. "When I asked him why he gave up so fucking easily. Why he let me take the reins, even though the only reason anyone followed me and not Sergei was because of him. He became a shadow of who he was, Rose. Maybe for the better, but…he was still broken."

"What did he say?"

"He told me about a woman he knew." He sounds distant, as if he's relaying some sordid fairytale he hasn't deciphered yet. "A woman who showed him what love was." He laughs and I doubt it was a cherished lesson. "He said it was like a rose. Beautiful, but painful. The thorns dig deep. They cut through you, but a part of you still won't let it go."

"Is that the real reason why you call me Rose?" I ask in a thready whisper. "To mock me?"

"To warn myself," he replies. "I always fucking knew… You'd cut me into pieces."

"I want to trust you." My hand goes to my stomach before I can help it. At the moment, it's flat, seemingly empty. "I need to trust you. So stop pushing me away every time I try."

"I will… But I need you to promise me—right fucking now." He turns me to face him, his eyes like midnight. "You won't ever use this against me." He gestures to my belly. "That you won't ever turn against me."

My lips part, but it's a promise I'm not brave enough to make just yet. All I can do is take his hand, intertwining my fingers with his. "Learn to trust me and I won't ever have a reason to betray you."

"Trust." He leans in, mulling over the word like it's a foreign concept. "I'm sure that includes many avenues we can build on. Thoroughly. Maybe we'll live out that fantasy yet."

My cheeks flame as I recall his vision of the future: me, giving him multiple children.

"But first..." He draws back suddenly serious. "I'm going to drive the nightmares from your skull. For good."

Meaning Robert Winthorp and this stupid, petty war. Did my mother know the chaos she'd leave in her wake with such a simple lie?

As Vanya stated, Mischa doesn't even know the extent.

"How?" I ask.

He hesitates and I can see the war within himself playing out across his features. Hatred and desire. Finally, something wins. "We're going to cut the serpent off at its head."

In other words: kill Robert.

"When?"

"Soon." He stares off into the distance. "Fairly soon."

"And when it happens, you'll tell me?"

"Yes." He looks down, meeting my gaze. "I'll tell you, Little Rose. As promised, I'll even let you twist the knife."

CHAPTER 20

Mischa seems to think I hate Robert—enough to want him dead—but I'm not sure if that's the case. Can you hate someone who merely exploited a willing victim?

Everything he did was never forced—even the supposed death of our child.

I just never questioned. Like a good doll, I merely accepted every explanation he deigned to toss my way.

You can't blame a wolf for devouring a doe.

But you can blame a monster cunning enough to deceive his prey. One who enjoys watching his victims squirm in anguish. After all, the wolf only seeks to sate a primal urge, but the monster?

He desires control above all else. Power.

And, for whatever reason, the only man to come to mind in that context is Sergei.

He finally makes his reappearance as Mischa and I return to the manor as the first hints of darkness creep along the horizon.

"I need to speak with you," he says, meeting us at the edge of the gardens. Though he speaks to us both, his eyes remain fixated on me. "In private, if you please."

"Why?" Mischa demands. He steps forward, effortlessly inserting himself in between us. "Is there something you can't say in my presence, Sergei?"

"No," the man says calmly. "But I am sure there are some things that Ellen would not like discussed. Even in front of you." He turns and beckons me with a nod. "I'll be in the drawing room off the foyer."

Mischa starts after him, but I place a hand on his shoulder.

"I'll be fine."

When I enter the manor without him, I can sense his ever-present hesitation. Once again, his paranoia will fester. Can he truly trust me?

I can't bring myself to look back and gauge which emotion wins out.

Instead, I force my shoulders back and navigate my way to Sergei alone. Sure enough, I find him in a large room lined with bookshelves. He's standing near a row of windows, glaring out at the dimming sky. It's easy to see the resemblance between him and Vanya now; they share the same contemplative, brown eyes and stern expression. But where Vanya radiates an exhausted neutrality, Sergei is always alert. Always watching.

"That was a remarkable performance the other night," he praises, but I suspect that the compliment is more grudging than genuine. "You reminded me so much of—"

"Marnie?" I interject. My arms go around my chest. It's instinct. A subconscious guarding against the cold shift in his posture. He's standing taller, angled away from me.

It's like he knows the topic on my mind before I even voice it.

"Why didn't you tell me that she wasn't taken? She *willingly* left the Winthorps."

"Ivan told you that?" he scoffs dismissively. "Always the romantic—"

"So then what is the truth?" I'm too tired to disguise the pain in my voice. "Just tell me."

"Fine." He faces me, crossing his arms as well. "You deserve to hear it. Your mother wasn't the naïve innocent that rumor and legend have turned her into. She was a cunning, intelligent, and—I'll say it—ruthless young woman. The elder Winthorp forced her into marriage—did she tell you that?"

I lick my lips, unsure of just how much I should reveal. I'm on a different playing field than the battles I've fought with

Mischa. There are no petty tricks or scathing insults to dodge. Sergei reminds me of a tactician, already twenty steps ahead, one wrong move from instant checkmate.

"She didn't tell me much about her family," I admit.

In reality, she told me nothing.

"Oh?" A satisfied gleam flits across his gaze, but the instant I place it, it's already gone. "Do you know that the Winthorps liked to dip into the sex trade? Your mother was one of those unfortunate girls, plucked from obscurity, destined to be sold to some rich, old baron. Unfortunately, Robert Winthorp took a liking to her first. She was undeniably beautiful..." He trails off as if staring into the past, seeing her, this lovely, doomed creature. "But she was far smarter than the bastard gave her credit for. She tricked him into believing she loved him despite the circumstances of their meeting. So he married her. Worshipped the ground she walked on, and gradually, she convinced him to grant her more and more freedom until she could enter and leave the manor as she pleased."

In some ways, the woman he's described sounds more like Briar than Marnie: cunning to her own advantage.

"So why did she come to you?"

"Me?" He raises an eyebrow. "No, she went to *Ivan*. He was the liaison between the *mafiya* and the Winthorps."

"They did your accounts," I recall from what Mischa told me—but he never mentioned that *Vanya* oversaw that little arrangement. "In return, you protected their investments."

"Yes." His eyebrows furrow. Is he surprised I know as much? "Marnie went to Ivan with a proposition: She would tell him everything she knew about the Winthorp business if he rescued her and her daughter."

"So there was no kidnapping." I can't tell if the hitch in my voice is due to shock or relief. "The whole start of this war was based on a lie—"

"Not quite," Sergei corrects. "Winthorp was growing bolder. He planned to attack us eventually and control our territory himself. By warning Ivan, Marnie thought she was saving his life. She was also sly enough to ensure she got something out of it."

Could the mother I knew truly be that selfless? And simultaneously selfish?

"So then what happened?" I prompt.

"Ivan came to me with her plan and I agreed to use my resources to assist in her escape. But, in the end, Briar was left behind."

Something pinches in my chest. Jealousy? I know it's selfish to feel it now. But a cruel part of my mind eagerly points out the glaring facts I want to ignore. Marnie sacrificed her freedom for Briar, but in return, she doomed me to a lifetime of hell. Did the fact that Vanya was my father make it easier for her to live with such a choice?

Maybe, as Mischa believed, her love had been a lie.

"How was she recaptured?" I ask, returning to the topic at hand.

"I don't know." Sergei meets my gaze, but I can't discern a single emotion from his expression. "When she had a child roughly nine months later, I suspected that you were Ivan's."

"So why didn't you tell him?"

He stiffens and eyes the knuckles of his hand. One by one, he curls each finger into a fist. A ring glints from one of them: silver, sporting the visage of a coiled serpent.

"Tell him what? That the woman he loved turned her back on him? That she would rather raise his bastard among the Winthorps than send her to her father? How could I tell my brother that?"

My chest tightens with the weight of such a twisted dilemma. I couldn't imagine making a decision at all—but I've had twenty-four years to live with the consequences of his.

"So you left me there."

"With your mother," he corrects. "And when she died... I didn't know your circumstances were as dire as they were. How could I?"

But something in me won't accept that answer. "You told Mischa that I was the continuation of your line." At least before Anna was found. "You said you knew about me since the day I was born. For someone who seems to care so much about your family, you have an odd way of showing it."

"And I deserve your anger, yes." He nods. "I deserve your mistrust, even. But for a second, think from your mother's point of view. She kept you from your father, but perhaps that, more than anything, reveals her true thoughts of Ivan? Perhaps we were her pawns all along? After all, would you return your son to Robert Winthorp?"

"Don't." I cut off his scenario with a sharp wave of my hand. "Don't you dare mention him. I never had a choice in how he grew up."

"And if you could have done things differently?"

My heart breaks. "I would have never left him alone. Never."

Even if it meant putting on a charade with Robert.

"And maybe your mother felt differently than you in that respect," he says. "But now that you have been reunited with your son, what choice will you make?"

I grit my teeth at how effortlessly he's managed to turn the tables. "Why do you care?" A suspicion creeps into my brain as if on cue. "Could it be because he's the Winthorp heir? If Robert dies…"

Then Eli could stand to inherit it all.

"Maybe you should ask Mischa the same question?" Sergei steps forward and brushes his hand along my cheek. "It's not my place to poison you against him—"

"You couldn't," I counter, but my voice falls flat. A weakness he doesn't miss.

"I would caution you to carefully consider your circumstances. I didn't kidnap Marnie Winthorp. I never brutalized her or made her a martyr, but can Mischa say the same?" His thumb grazes my branded cheek for emphasis. "There are some lines even I won't cross. I wouldn't use your child against you, and when you realize that, we can further this discussion."

He moves past me for the door, but before he crosses the threshold, I call out, "You claim you wouldn't use children, but what about Briar Winthorp?"

"Briar." He stiffens with one foot still in the air. "What about her?"

Something in his tone makes me blurt my words out with no ounce of tact. "You were willing to have her killed when Anna-Natalia was taken. Weren't you?"

It sounds so evil when paired with Misha's supposed crimes. Ruthless.

But Sergei doesn't flinch. "What could I possibly gain from the death of a little girl?"

Without giving me the chance to ponder that, he leaves.

On the surface, he has a point.

But the answer doesn't take long for me to settle on. What could a man like him gain? Nothing material, perhaps. Not money or Winthorp prestige.

But I know firsthand what the death of a child could do to a woman.

You could break her irreparably.

You could change her loyalties.

And perhaps the cruelest aim of all: you could punish her.

CHAPTER 21

My room is a quiet refuge after my conversation with Sergei—but not for long. The second I lift my dress over my head, I hear the door open.

Cool air drifts in, ushering heavy footsteps. Alarmed, I cover my chest with my hands—but maybe the act is for show. Because I can identify my intruder by his scent alone.

"You don't look very pregnant," he declares, eyeing me up and down. "And I would like to think that I would notice."

"Is that so?" I turn away from him, eyeing my reflection flung over the window. "I haven't menstruated since I've been with you," I admit, smoothing my hand along my abdomen. "And…I just know."

His steps echo as he comes up behind me. "And now?" he wonders near my ear. "Do I treat you like a glass doll? No more sex?"

The scary part is how earnest he sounds. Curious.

"Would this really stop you?" I press my hand against my flat stomach as if shielding innocent ears from his answer.

"Maybe," he admits, surprising me. "But that doesn't mean I can't touch you. Watch you." He grabs my waist, guiding me against him. "I think I could enjoy that."

Closing my eyes, I let my head fall back against his shoulder. "I hate the way you toy with me." I sound pained. Desperate.

"I hate the way you tempt me." In retaliation, he runs his finger beneath my rib cage. Then he guides me to face him. "It's like you're a witch." He laughs bitterly at his own descriptor as he startles me by sinking to his knees. "It's the truth. You make me feel things, Rose… Devious little things. I've wanted to kill men before, but never like what I want to do to you."

"Oh?" I shiver as his fingers brush the backs of my knees, urging me closer.

"Yes." He nods, but against me, the motion feels more like a caress. "I want to destroy you. Devour you."

"You sound like you want to hurt me—" I break off as his lips ghost my abdomen and flutter over my hip bones. My knees tremble. For stability, I sink my hands into his hair.

"Painfully. That's how I crave you," he whispers. "There is no sanity. No logic. When I'm with you, I crave every fucking thing I spent years telling myself I never wanted."

Mischa Stepanov deny himself anything? "Like what?"

"More," he admits, fanning his hands over my belly. "More than the *mafiya*. More than crushing Winthorp. You make me consider a life beyond it all. And I never wanted to before."

Because this violence and conflict are all he has.

"But I'm going to watch your belly swell, Rose," he promises between heavy breaths. "I'm going to watch you grow with my child. And…" He looks up, meeting my gaze. "And maybe I'll change my mind."

"About what?" I say, barely able to breathe.

He looks down and rests his forehead against me. "About it all. Maybe we could leave Winthorp behind. Runaway to that tiny strip of the world I know you've dreamt about. The place where violence and death can't follow you. Only those worthy of sharing such a paradise with. Anna, and Vanya, and Eli, and Mouse…"

"But you can't," I whisper, dashing the fantasy before it can unfold.

"Because this is who I am," he agrees, but for once, it's not a boast. "And one day you'll take your pretty eyes, and your baby, and your sweet little cunt, and you'll leave me, Rose. Men like me don't keep women like you for very long. Ask Ivan."

"Shut up." I curl my fingers in his hair and pull until a growl revs in his throat. "Just... Just tell me that you want me."

"Want," he chuckles and stands, trailing his lips up my torso the entire way. When he reaches my lips, he claims them, groaning at the taste. "I need you, Rose—but not like your precious husband did. You don't keep me sane, or human, or anything like that." He kisses me even deeper, guiding me into his arms. Against my parted lips, he says, "You make me *think* after years of hating, and killing, and feeling. I can finally fucking think."

And he makes that simple fact sound more powerful than any other commodity I've known men to chase.

Including any amount of money.

I wake up in Mischa's arms, but my first instinct isn't to squirm, or endure, or count down the seconds. I turn the tables instead and observe him in the pale light of dawn streaming in through the window. He's deeply asleep, lying on his back, with my body crushed to his side. Even unconscious, he's possessive.

I can't stop myself from touching him when he's like this. He's handsome while peaceful, irresistibly so. For a second, I toy with the idea of what his child might look like. Perpetually angry, with a head of wild hair? Would they have his dark eyes as well? Or maybe blue, like Eli's...

Sergei's warning intrudes on the innocent thought: Does Mischa intend to use him for his own gain?

I pull my hand away and it's like flipping a switch. Mischa opens his eyes, homing them on me. He shifts and captures my wrist, resettling my hand over the tattooed flesh above where his heart resides.

"See something you like, Rose?" he wonders, his voice husky.

"What do *you* see when you look at me?" I ask. "A pawn? A willing victim? Or is it leverage—"

He sighs and releases me. "Someone hasn't been paying attention."

I wait for him to shove me off and storm away, but he doesn't move. Neither do I. With my face against his chest, I can hear his heart beating. The steady, gentle thrum is my translator for whatever his face doesn't express. He may be wearing a shadow of a scowl, but he isn't angry.

He's...content. Such a strange concept that I have to feel it rather than observe. In him, peace is expressed in slow, heavy breathing and muscles that twitch only slightly when I run my fingers over them.

"Maybe I need to hear you say it out loud?" I counter, using his saying to my advantage.

"Hmm." He hums low in his throat and then looks down on me from across the scarred, tattooed planes of his chest. "Out loud... How about: Robert Winthorp begged for you the second I realized you weren't Briar? He offered millions to have you back. He even offered to trade his own sister. Then he killed his father with his bare hands. By then, you weren't of any use to me but as bait, so what reason would I have for keeping you?"

I mull over the question, trying to view the world as he does, where everyone has a price tag—even little girls who are intentionally silenced in order to play a role in some criminal enterprise.

"You could want to use me as a sex slave?" I venture to guess. "You did threaten to sell me."

He scoffs. "I beat Kostatantin Vorshev within an inch of his life—not because he was a lying cunt, selling me out to Winthorp. No... Because he touched you. He hurt you." He reaches out, dragging his fingers along my cheek. "I kept Mouse—not that I would ever sell her back to Nicolai—but I kept her here because she reminded me of you. You look at me the same fucking way: like you're waiting for the moment I'll pull out my knife and run you through." He laughs, but it's a hollow, empty sound. "And if you're worried about him. Your son..." He tilts his head back, eyeing the ceiling. "There is Robert Winthorp in him. I can see it. He can be ruthless when he plays." He laughs, and it's real this time. "He declared 'war' on the roses in the garden and decapitated an entire bush of them. That boy is definitely a Winthorp."

I stiffen, but not out of fear. It's the first time he's said that name with something other than hate lacing it: admiration?

"But he has more of you. His eyes. His laugh. As young as he is, he isn't afraid to show compassion or guilt. I think he'll grow up just fine, Rose."

I look away, blinking rapidly. "Thanks to Anna."

"No." He guides my chin into the palm of his hand, forcing me to meet his gaze. "Anna may be part of it, but some of it is you."

"And do you think you can use him in ways you're unwilling to use me?" I have to ask him.

He sighs. "I should be. I'm sure Robert would pay just as much or even more to have him back. But I'm a selfish fuck, Rose." He sits up, bringing me with him, and pushes the covers back. "He isn't going anywhere."

My heart swells, sensing the ruthless promise contained within that boast.

"Thank you," I rasp.

"But he's not the only reason you're worried," he suspects. "I've seen you watching me and Anna together."

I bite my lip, but the pain does little to counteract the flood of fire searing my cheeks. "You loved her. I can understand that—"

"I still do," he says. "But not how you think. We grew up together. In some ways, we were more like siblings than anything else. And if something more might have come from it…" He shrugs and slides his arm from around me.

Before I can mourn the loss of heat, his hand captures mine. "We will never know."

Letting me go, he stands and grabs his pants from the floor. "But, now, I need to ask *you* something. Sergei put that suspicion into your head. Didn't he?"

I briefly consider denying it—whatever is brewing between the two men, something warns me that it isn't good. In the end, I nod. "He said you might have 'plans' for him."

Mischa scoffs. "I might have plans… Do you trust him?"

The hostility in his tone stings. "I-I don't know—"

"I don't." He pulls his shirt on and starts to pace, speaking to me from over his shoulder. "The night you were taken—from right under his fucking nose, I might add—he put on a grand show, Sergei. But something was off."

I sit straighter, bracing my feet on the floor. "What do you mean?"

He could be giving in to paranoia, but I can't ignore my own suspicions. As much as I try to deny it, our escape was too damn easy.

"I know the man," Mischa says, frowning as he dissects his thoughts. "I know when he's worried. I know when he's afraid. But that night, he wasn't."

"What are you saying?"

"I'm saying: Watch the man for yourself. Listen to everything he says, and use that smart brain of yours, Rose."

He taps his finger on his forehead for emphasis. "I'd say I'm not a very complicated man. I plan directly and go for the jugular. But Sergei plays mind games. I warned you once and I will warn you again: He was the most effective and ruthless leader the *mafiya* had. Don't forget that. Now, get dressed." He tosses something to me that I barely manage to catch: my plain dress. "I want to show you something."

Whatever he aims to show me requires intruding on the small sitting room where Anna is cuddling with Eli. He's nestled on her lap while she hums a song and runs her fingers through his hair. Spotting us, she stiffens.

"I can go," I blurt, but she shakes her head.

"No." She stands and gingerly sets the boy on the floor. "Mischa." Her voice breaks, but she swallows and tries again. "I'd like to go for a walk, please."

"Of course." Mischa extends his hand to her and guides her to the doorway.

Looking back at Eli, Anna forces a pained smile. "You stay here, my darling. I'll be just a moment, all right?"

Eli shrugs, wringing his fingers.

As they leave, I sit on the chair beside him. "My name is Ellen," I say. Of all the ways to begin this conversation, it's the only one to come to mind.

I wonder if Robert ever told him as much.

To my surprise, he nods solemnly and digs something from beneath the collar of his crisp blue shirt. His locket. Mischa must have returned it to him. With his tiny fingers, he pries it open and holds it up for my inspection.

I barely recognize the woman staring blankly from a small color photo. Angel, he called her? More like a ghost. Her blue eyes are lifeless, her face unblemished. I can't even recall a time such a picture could have been taken—it's as if my entire life before now has been a blur. Snippets of clarity in the midst of a nightmare.

But him...

I never forgot him, no matter how hard I tried.

Gingerly, I brush my finger along his cheek. It's plump, sporting twin dimples and a ruddy redness. The boyish attributes soften the reality of his slender neck and elegant nose—Winthorp features.

Even now, a part of me half expects him to fade beneath my fingertips—this is all some cruel fantasy.

But he doesn't.

Beaming, he points to a pile of objects strewn over the floor instead. Someone found him makeshift toys: a spoon, a small ball, and a porcelain figurine far too delicate to have been intended for use by a child.

"Watch," he commands. Flopping onto his stomach, he smashes the spoon against the ball.

And I observe him for what feels like an eternity, my eyes watering.

Robert kept me caged for years, and despite Mischa's insistence to the contrary, I don't think I hate him for it. I can't.

Because as cruel as he was, I *let* him use, and control, and manipulate me. I made myself numb to every bit of abuse and fed myself the lie that survival was worth it.

But this? My throat aches as I picture what life could have been like just for a second if I had Eli. I would have looked upon his innocent face and maybe I would have seen through the bars of my narrow cage for the first time. I would have known that no future was worth suffering an existence where he would see his father as a monster and his mother as a victim.

Holding Eli back then, I would have woken up from the dazed, nightmarish life Robert had accustomed me to.

And he knew it. Just like Mischa manipulates his own pawns across this ruthless gameboard, Robert maneuvered me and his own son as well. All in the name of leverage, and power, and winning.

But this is one game I can't excuse him for playing.

And this crime deserves more than death as a punishment.

*A*nna and Mischa return far too soon, with Mouse in tow. Eli jumps to his feet when he spots the younger girl, and the two promptly dash into the hallway, playing a makeshift game of chase.

"Outside," Mischa bellows and the children heed his command with him grumbling in their wake.

"Shall we make sure no one loses an eye?" Anna asks. For once, her small smile seems genuine.

Together, we enter the gardens and find the children darting between the trees while Mischa stands guard nearby. From here, his stern shouts are easily discernible.

"You have five minutes to hide. After that…I will be taking prisoners."

My heart swells while I watch him. Even if I still have doubts about his plans for me or Eli, I know one thing more than anything else: He'll make a good father.

If this war doesn't consume him first.

So lost in thought, I barely hear Anna say, "It feels so strange to be out in the fresh air again."

I turn and find the wind whipping her hair behind her as if in emphasis.

"Visiting the gardens once every few days was a rare treat," she says.

My heart pangs. I recognize the wistful note in her voice. Once upon a time, I might have said the same thing.

"I'm sorry," I tell her. "If I had known…"

I'm not sure what I could have done. Warned Mischa at least. He could have rescued her sooner.

"Don't," she says softly. "In a selfish way, I almost wish I had more time with…" She shakes her head and clears her throat. "Mischa told me what Robert told you. That Eli —*Robert*—was dead. And as horrible as it sounds, I almost wish you *had* abandoned him. I would feel less guilty."

"You shouldn't. He's beautiful. And Eli is a wonderful name." Watching him, I'm struck by a sudden realization. Perhaps *this* is what Mischa wanted to show me: a young boy with wild, blond hair traipsing boldly through the edge of the forest.

There is no mistaking the hints of Robert Winthorp peeking from his features. His nose. His mouth. The calculating way he eyes his target—Mouse—before pouncing on her without warning. But he's quicker to laugh, and his impish grin reflects no ounce of malice.

Robert Winthorp may be his father, but he is his own person.

And I have hope that he will be different.

For better *or* for worse.

CHAPTER 23

Mischa runs the children ragged until they barely have the strength to make it to the upstairs sitting room before collapsing into respective corners.

"I'll get them some water," Anna suggests. Smiling, she hustles toward the stairs.

Funnily enough, even Mischa looks winded. He pants while meeting my gaze and rakes the sweat-soaked hair from his face. "What are you thinking behind those judging little eyes, Rose?"

I turn away, spotting Eli curled on his side, deeply asleep. Across from him, poor Mouse is struggling to keep her eyes open. The dirt and mud streaking their faces are clues as to the kind of "games" they were playing.

"I'm thinking that you have a very strange idea of playtime."

Knife fighting, war drills, and escape lessons.

"And what should we be doing instead?" Mischa asks, crossing his arms. "Playing with dollies and tea parties?"

"Maybe."

He frowns. "Maybe it's you that has a strange idea of playtime."

"If all you teach them is violence and war, then all you can see in their future is violence and war," I explain, gesturing toward Mouse. She's fully asleep now, huddled against the wall, but her posture remains tense. Guarded. As if she expects an attack at any moment. "And maybe it's naïve, and foolish, and stupid, but…"

"What?" he prods when I fall silent. I look over, surprised by the stern tilt to his jaw. He's curious.

"I think it's braver to imagine a future for them in which their only fear is pouring the tea wrong or wearing an outdated dress to dinner. Is that so wrong?"

Maybe it is—shallow in a sense.

But while I always resented Briar's vain upbringing, there was a comfort in it that I envied more than anything.

She never had to evade her father's men or jump on the first offer of security thrown her way. She never saw safety as a commodity worth trading her soul for.

"I don't want to fear for them." I brush my hand along my stomach before I can help it. "I'd rather *hope* for them."

"And what does hope lie in?" he counters, though I don't think he's mocking me. His tone is way too soft. "Piano lessons and etiquette classes?"

I shrug. "Maybe. Or in someplace where they can feel safe. A home. One they don't have to worry might be invaded—"

"Rose." His posture shifts and he becomes the imposing soldier once more.

I turn to the doorway and see why. Sergei stands there, flanked by Vanya.

"Sorry to interrupt," the older man says. Dressed in black, he radiates an authority even Mischa reacts to by gritting his teeth. "But something has come up that may draw your interest."

"What is it?" Mischa demands.

"Since Ellen decided our course of action, I think I may have the perfect opportunity in mind for you to fulfill it."

Mischa stiffens. "Fine. But then she can hear the details as well." He gestures toward me with a wave of his hand.

"Of course." Sergei extends his arm in a silent invitation to follow. "I don't object."

"I'll stay here," Anna suggests, appearing beside her father. Her eyes go to Eli and she smiles. "If I can wake them up, I'll send the children off to bed."

"Fine." Mischa shoulders past me and enters the hall. "Let's hear it, then."

"As you wish." Sergei pulls ahead and descends the stairs. Leading the way, he approaches the larger drawing room off the foyer.

Mischa and Vanya form a guarded audience along the wall while Sergei stands in the middle.

"After the unceremonious death of his father, Robert Winthorp has had to shore up support among the old man's allies," Sergei says. "Some of them, admittedly, are wary about an untested upstart. I know for a fact that Robert is on his way to one of those men as we speak. Unfortunately for him, I have my men staked along the route as well."

"So an ambush," Mischa surmises, stroking his chin. Raw hunger for revenge sinks into the line of his mouth, tilting it at the corner. His eyes, however, remain mistrustful. "And what is your plan?"

"Simple," Sergei replies. "I'll provide support. You and your men can have your prize. I won't interfere."

"Oh?" A tense few seconds pass as Mischa rattles off various logistics at a rapid-fire pace.

When.

Where.

How.

Sergei has an answer for every one.

Finally, Mischa sighs and drags his fingers through his hair, raking the strands back from his face. "So when do we go?"

"Now."

As if on cue, a man appears in the doorway. Though he isn't wearing the crisp, black ensemble most of Sergei's men do, I don't recognize him as Mischa's, either. Plain jeans and a short-sleeved tee-shirt set him apart, as do a few scattered tattoos down the length of his arms. One in particular draws my interest: a serpent coiled around a cross.

"This is one of my best scouts," Sergei says, drawing my attention back to him. "He will be your liaison as we bring up the rear."

"You won't be with us?" Vanya asks.

"I think it's for the best if Mischa takes the lead in this instance," Sergei replies, eyeing the younger man thoughtfully. "I wouldn't want to interfere."

"But shouldn't we call another council? Discuss this with the other heads? Request support—"

"You worry too much, Ivan," Sergei interjects.

"Does he though?" Mischa cocks his head as if a sudden thought occurred to him. "It isn't like you to be rash, Sergei."

"Rash?" The man strokes his chin. "Or prudent? After all, the best way to catch your enemy is off guard. However, I will concede to convening with the heads. It's unusual to meet so soon after a council—"

"But we'll make an exception," Mischa says. His eyes cut in my direction, impossible to read. "Little Rose should learn the true ways of the *mafiya*."

"Infernal politics," Vanya grumbles.

"Though necessary," Sergei says. "What say you, Mischa?"

"Fine. I'll arrange a *banquet*." He puts a mocking twist on the term. "For tomorrow night. From there, we can discuss our next course of action."

Both brothers nod in unison. "Agreed."

"Good." Mischa pulls away from the wall, but on his way out, he grabs my arm, dragging me after him.

In silence, he leads me past the staircase and into another room. One that, I assume, was chosen at random. It's spacious, but instead of portraits on the walls, this one sports weapons locked behind glass. Knives. Guns.

It's like being inside Mischa's brain.

"So what do you think?" the man in question murmurs against my ear. "Should we trust the charming Sergei Vasilev?"

He grunts when I don't give him an answer—but I'm still stuck on his use of that dangerous term. *We.*

"Tell me, Rose—"

"I don't know," I admit. "But you don't."

His mouth tightens as if his first instinct is to deny it. Then he shrugs. "You saw something. When Sergei's muscle came in. Your face changed."

"What?" I recall the unfamiliar man, picturing him clearly in my head. "I don't…"

"What?" he demands as I feel my face pale. "What is it?"

"I think…" My blood runs cold as I picture his tattoo. A serpent and cross. I've seen it before just once. My eyes widen as I meet Mischa's intent stare. "I think he's the man I saw outside of the hotel. When Anna and I escaped."

"What?" Mischa's eyebrows furrow. "No, it's…"

"Insane," I agree, my voice hoarse. "I must have seen it wrong."

"No." He sighs, gritting his teeth. "It's fucking devious and calculating. No wonder the bastard wasn't worried."

He apparently had a man on the inside.

"Do you think he's working with Robert?" Even as I voice such a suggestion, it sounds too fantastical to consider.

"I don't know," Mischa admits. "What was that spiel of yours about hope again? Maybe the raw, honest truth is that there is no such thing. You can delude yourself into thinking as much in a moment of weakness." He drags a finger along my cheek. "But then you find a knife in your back."

"Are you trying to warn me?" I ask, though I'm honestly not sure if I'm brave enough to hear the answer.

"Maybe," he admits. His breath ghosts my lips and I realize just how close he is: towering above me with a hairsbreadth between us. "Or maybe you've already realized that." He nods to my abdomen and the hand I have protectively braced there. "Either way… It's time for you to play some games my way."

"Like how?"

His nod beckons for me to follow as he crosses to the other end of the room. Two leather chairs are positioned at opposite corners. Mischa claims one for himself, leaving the other for me.

"Sit," he commands while he does the same, letting his bulk strain the confines of the leather.

The casualness is all for show, I suspect. When I meet his gaze, it's honed like a razor, deadly serious.

"So what will we play?" I force myself to ask.

"A history lesson." He props his elbow on his knee and then perches his chin atop the same hand. "The most dangerous game of all. Navigating a room of murderers and cutthroats —while gaining something from it at the same time. Let's say that Sergei is a snake, and that he's planning something…" He clenches his jaw, and his knuckles are white over the armrest from gripping it so tightly. "Then the only way to beat him is to anticipate him. Outmaneuver him. Outsmart him. Do you think you have what it takes?"

I eye him from head to toe, unnerved by what I find now. An unguarded Mischa offering up more secrets.

Forget the knife. *This* is the most dangerous weapon in his arsenal.

Trust.

"Do I? I don't know," I admit, supplying an answer before he can. "But I can learn. So teach me."

"Good." He smiles and a part of me squirms in anticipation. How strange it feels to finally be included in one of his schemes. "First, a bit of advice. Men like Sergei are patient. They can get inside your head and outwit any plan before you even come up with it. How do you defeat a man like that?"

"How?" In a way, dealing with him has given me the answer. I don't think Mischa realizes how similar he is to his old mentor. And the few times I've ever fought back against him have been born from the same place. "You can't plan," I say, frowning.

Mischa raises an eyebrow, but he doesn't interject even though I've just contradicted his entire argument. "Oh? How, then."

I shrug. "You just have to react. Intuitively."

Like starving yourself out of spite due to an insult.

Or attacking someone, claws drawn, when they expect you to surrender.

Desperation is the only tactic that can't be outmaneuvered.

"There is no way to outwit someone like that," I say, meeting Mischa's probing stare. "You can only retaliate."

"Hmph." He chuckles deeply, but there's no mocking in his tone. Admiration instead? "*Now*, you are thinking like a member of the *mafiya*. So tell me, Rose: How do you plan to react to him?"

*M*afiya history lessons seem more like horror stories. Murderers who command respect through their gruesome deeds. Drug smugglers. Politicians who deal in lies. The insights haunt me all night, circling my brain until morning comes.

Mischa plans his "banquet" with little fanfare. It's almost insulting compared to something one might have found at Winthorp Manor in its heyday. There are no four-course meals planned or tables draped in finery. In fact, the meal itself seems secondary to the true main course: intrigue.

"There," Mischa says against the nape of my neck. "Watch them. Do you remember your lesson?"

We stand positioned near a window overlooking the front of the manor. The setting sun reflects off a row of black vehicles lined up in the courtyard like children's toys.

One by one, various figures exit them.

"There's Boris Lynchkoft," Mischa remarks, referring to a balding man in a tight suit being ushered from a limo by two men who I assume are bodyguards. "And he…"

"Runs a drug trade," I rasp, recalling my "history lesson." "He isn't loyal to Sergei per se, but he doesn't like you, either."

"Good. And him?" He points to a different man exiting a dark sports car this time, flanked by even more muscle.

"Andrei Zagitov," I say. "He launders money through a shipping operation he owns. Also a somewhat neutral party. Him, along with Alexi Somodorov," I add, nodding to a different man strolling up the stone path to the manor's entrance. With a head of silver hair, he's the oldest man of the bunch. "He controls mercenaries and makes up the last party whose alliances you're unsure of."

"Very good." Mischa flicks his thumb along my chin, guiding my face toward him. In his eyes, I see something that may be amusement. He isn't scowling for once, either. "You may be able to play the game yet, Rose. But…" He cuts his eyes down to my dress—one of the few from the wardrobe in my room—and frowns. "Not like this."

"Oh?" I smooth my hands along the cotton skirt. "I never knew you had such an interest in fashion."

"Fashion?" He scoffs. "It's presentation. The wolf can't show up to the den dressed like a sheep."

"I didn't know you were poetic, either," I remark dryly.

"You don't know a lot of things about me, Rose. But I do have a feeling that Sergei won't supply you with a dress this time. At least not one fit for a wolf."

He takes my hand, leading me back through the upstairs level of the manor and into my room.

Sure enough, a dress is waiting for me, draped over the end of my bed.

But I doubt Sergei had a hand in choosing it.

"I guess wolves wear red in your world?" I croak, breathless.

Mischa cups my waist, guiding me back against his chest. "*This* wolf," he murmurs near my ear. "She is cunning and sly, and she bathes in the blood of those foolish enough to trust her." I stiffen, but he brushes his lips along my throat, negating any insult his words may contain. "Put it on."

With him on my heels, I approach the bed and run my fingers along the garment: a silk gown composed of a stunning shade of scarlet.

"It's beautiful—"

"Here." Mischa helps me shed my dress and ease the new one over my head.

Spotting my reflection in a nearby mirror, I certainly don't look like my mother.

Or Briar.

I'm someone new, clothed in blood red that highlights her healing wounds and injuries. Paired with the man beside me, I don't resemble a captive, either.

"Your necklace." Mischa runs his fingers along my neck, highlighting the absence of my rose charm. "It's gone—"

"Robert took it." I brush my fingers along the hollow spot as my heart pangs. The one thing I may have had of Marnie's, lost. "But I'm sure that means nothing to you. Mr. 'there is no point in getting attached to things.'"

"You're right," he agrees. "Only a fool would ever think there was something meaningful in some worthless trinket."

My face heats, but the second I try to pull away, he grabs my shoulder. I jump as something tickles my collar. When I look down, my eyes go wide.

"So consider me a fool, then," he grumbles while manipulating a slender, golden chain in one hand.

I gape as he fastens it around my neck. It's longer than the other one, sporting a delicate charm that takes my breath away: a rose in full bloom.

"It's lovely," I whisper, brushing my fingers along the charm. "I don't know what to—"

"Enough."

I sense him lean into me, his mouth in my hair, his breathing slow and heavy.

With my free hand, I reach back and find one of his, clenching tight. My body relaxes into him, fitting neatly within the rugged contours that make up his bulk. When I feel a telltale hardness against my hip, I press against him, drawing a groan from his lips.

"No." He pulls back, sliding his hands down my thighs until the last possible second. "If you tempt me now, we'll be late..."

I turn and find him eyeing me from head to toe, his eyelids lowered.

"*Very* late." When he bites his lip, I know he's mulling over that very possibility, weighing the pros and cons. Then he sighs. Apparently, politics trumps all else.

Even sex.

"But. First, my wolf needs to bare her teeth." He positions me with my back to him and runs his fingers through my hair. Within seconds, it's arranged into an elegant coil.

"And now what?" I ask as he observes his handiwork, finally satisfied.

"Now, we enter the den." He extends his hand and captures one of mine. "But, this time, we remain as allies."

If I am a wolf, then Sergei resembles a bear. Approaching him head-on would be suicide, and the man relishes in his obvious strength. Once again, we're gathered in the grand hall. The marble floors magnify every sound, making those of us here—fifty at most—sound like hundreds.

Sergei holds court near the back of the room, surrounded by those of the council I recognize as having supported him at the last gathering. A black suit helps him cast an imposing aura damn near everyone succumbs to—Mischa included.

His grip tightens over my forearm, keeping me close to his side. Then he seems to realize his reaction and gradually loosens his grasp until we're standing apart entirely.

"This is an arena you'll have to navigate on your own, Rose," he murmurs as if reading my mind.

Childish panic goads my heart into beating faster. "What happened to us still being allies this time?" I demand, eyeing his clenched jaw. "Changed your mind already?"

"No. But every wolf needs to learn to hunt." His hand brushes my lower back, providing subtle reassurance while nudging me forward. "So hunt."

Before I can turn around, he's gone, slipping to the back of the room to strike up a conversation with a figure not mentioned in his "history lesson."

Alone, I spot Sergei already mingling with two of my three targets. The only remaining figure to approach happens to be the most intimidating enigma on my list, per Mischa: Alexi Somodorov.

He stands, eyeing a portrait hanging near the center of the room, his back to all other inhabitants.

Supposedly this man is second only to Sergei in terms of sheer ruthlessness. He murdered plenty of Winthorp associates, adding to the victim tally of this twisted war.

I approach him slowly as fear gnaws away at what little resolve I have. Hunt, Mischa told me.

But in what instance?

My role is nothing more than a formality. What power could a battered wife and illegitimate bastard truly command among such men?

"Look who deigns to grace me with her presence?"

Startled, I realize I've drawn even with Somodorov already.

He acknowledges my presence with a hiss, his eyes casting me a dismissive glance. "Robert Winthorp's whore."

I swallow hard as fire paints my cheeks. A part of me bristles at the insult, and I know what Mischa would do if he overheard: flex his muscle. Demand obedience.

But I am not him.

Tilting my head back, I meet the man's gaze directly, forcing him to maintain the eye contact far longer than comfortable. After all, only a coward would dare look away from a whore.

"I guess that means I know him better than anyone," I counter, surprised by how little my voice wavers. "Doesn't it?"

The man grunts and returns his attention to his painting. It depicts an ancient battlefield, where blood and mud churn in a sickening mass beneath fighting soldiers.

"I suppose so. But make no mistake, girl. I am not one of the besotted fools who think you may have some worth. Mischa called this little party for a reason. What?"

"No reason," I admit. "I simply wanted to learn."

"Oh?"

"I wanted to see for myself if any of you men truly have anything more to offer the world than someone like Robert Winthorp?"

His eyes flash and I know I'm on dangerous ground. Mischa relies on brute strength, Sergei on cunning, but what kind of combatant am I?

Neither, I'm realizing.

My strength may lie in something between the two. A skill that only a "whore" might possess and be willing to wield to its full potential. Something within my grasp, even now as Robert waits for me beyond these walls and secrets threaten the fragile security around me.

I excel at utilizing desperation.

To an artform.

"Tell me," Somodorov demands. "Why the hell should I entertain a child who got her say by fucking the head of the table? What could you possibly offer me?"

"It's simple." I copy him, observing the painting as well. In a way, it's a physical manifestation of our conversation. Mindless and static, mainly for show. The outcome is already set in stone: an eternal stalemate. "I can't offer you anything. Yet. But I think you know better than I do how alliances can change and that power can shift on a whim."

"Oh?" He laughs deep in his throat. "I don't have time for this—"

"Let me put it this way." I raise my voice just enough to stop him in his tracks. "You control mercenaries, correct? Who stands to lose more if the war with the Winthorps is over?"

"I have more important matters than Mischa's squabbles," the man scoffs.

"Fair enough. But then who might stand to see you as a threat if Robert is gone entirely? I don't think Mischa would care, but what about someone who may want to ensure they keep control of Winthorp estate themselves?"

He frowns and I instinctively brace. I'm on a tightrope. One wrong move and the consequences will be swift and brutal.

"Are you even suggesting what I think you are?"

"Of course not." I innocently incline my head. "But maybe your thoughts go in the same direction as mine? Some men would do anything to maintain their power. But a whore? All she would want is…peace."

Beyond his shoulder I find Mischa, watching us, his face unreadable.

"Excuse me." I slip past Somodorov, my heart pounding.

"I see you went for the most dangerous prey out of the gate," Mischa remarks once I reach him. The gruffness of his voice contrasts the odd tilt to his mouth betraying an emotion he's trying to resist: admiration. "He must like you. Alexi tends to stab what offends him." He eyes my throat, finding it unscathed. "What did you say to him?"

"Nothing," I rasp. "But I'm not sure I want to be a wolf for very long."

Not because I'm scared.

But because…

Toying the line between caution and power, I enjoyed every second of it.

I enjoyed it way too much.

CHAPTER 24

We move to the manor's expansive dining room, where the heavy atmosphere should lessen somewhat. However, when Sergei claims the head of the table, his stern expression reveals that this setting is yet another battlefield.

This line of fighting is a lot simpler, however.

A vote.

"Do we take our chance now?" he wonders, glancing around the table brimming with guests. "Or squander it?"

He looks to Mischa, but for once, the younger man seems reluctant to take the reins of the conversation. He sits sideways on the chair beside mine, his hand on his chin.

"I vote yes," another man pitches in from Sergei's end of the table. "I say we put an end to this now."

"Agreed," another man says.

"Fine." Mischa looks up, meeting Sergei's gaze directly. "I may have the final say, but old Sergei…he would never lead us astray."

"Then it's settled. We move out tonight."

"Tonight?" The question comes from Somodorov. "Launch a full-scale operation on Winthorp with just a few hours' notice? That seems hasty, Sergei."

"Or intuitive, he will be returning from his meeting," the other man corrects. "As Mischa stated, would I suggest a plan I didn't think would work?"

"I guess," Somodorov says, "but still. I think we—"

"We should vote," Mischa says over him. He lifts his hand, displaying the callused palm. "I say yes."

I bite my lip to disguise my shock. Has he changed his opinion so soon? Around the table, various sounds of agreement or dissent are voiced, but within minutes, a consensus is clear.

"Then it's settled," Sergei says. "We strike tonight. A small contingent. My men and Mischa's—"

"What about mine?" Alexi interjects.

"I think a smaller team is better," Sergei says. "We can be discreet until it's time to strike."

The men on his side of the table grumble in affirmation of that plan.

"Fine." Mischa stands and heads for the doorway. "We'll leave at midnight." Before he exits the room, his eyes cut to mine, brimming with a silent invitation to follow.

When I finally track him down, he's in the upstairs sitting room with his back to me. From another room, giggles erupt and I marvel at the innocent contrast to the grim discussion that took place below. Mouse and Eli are in their own universe, blissfully unaware of the danger brewing around them.

And I'd give my soul to keep them there.

"I don't trust it," Mischa admits as I advance on his position. "And I know you don't, either." He reaches out, grasping my hand. "But you can't show it. Not to him and not now."

"This doesn't sound like you." Cocking my head, I place my hands on my hips. "Mischa Stepanov, biding his time?"

His lips quirk almost too quickly to catch. "Maybe your pretty little words are stuck in my brain," he counters. "Peace. Fighting Sergei out in the open certainly won't achieve that. It would split the *mafiya* right down the fucking middle and start an even bloodier war than the one with Winthorp. If he is a fucking liar, I need him to prove it on his own."

Even if waiting kills him.

"You're right." I brush my hand along his shoulder, feeling the muscle flex at my touch. "There is a lot I don't know about you."

And maybe it's not a bad thing.

"But," I add, "if you don't confront him now, then when?"

He looks away, eyeing the world beyond the windows. "When the timing is right."

"And until then?"

He rakes his gaze down the length of me, tracing the plunging neckline of the dress. His fingers cinch a handful of silk, and it's no match, easily giving him enough leverage to lift it over my head.

"Mischa!" I gasp as he tugs me against him, fully naked. "Anyone could come in," I whisper, painfully aware of the faint giggles betraying a world beyond this room. As his mouth comes to nuzzle my throat, the danger feels farther and farther away. "We can't—"

His lips capture mine, silencing my protests. Grunting, he spins me around, pressing my body against the window. The thin sill provides just enough stability to support me as he draws back, tugging on the fastenings of his pants.

Seeing him bare in the dim light shouldn't be enough to make all logic dissipate from my brain. Straining and swollen, he's breathtaking. My fingers reach for him before I can help it, easing a groan from his lips.

"Be a different animal for now, my wolf," he murmurs, sinking inside me on a single thrust. "Something quiet," he grates as his eyes flutter closed. He groans again, his throat cording as he starts to move. "A sheep?"

I'm too breathless to mount a comeback. Each thrust is rough, plunging as deep as he possibly can without hurting me. This isn't for pleasure.

It's a promise.

A plea.

A demand.

"Mine," he grunts against my ear in time with his next punishing thrust. "You're mine, Rose. Say it."

"Yours," I breathe into his sweat-coated skin. My fingers trace the line of his throat, tracking the sharp inhalation he takes. "I'm yours… And you're mine."

He grunts in acknowledgment, bucking his hips. The full weight of my ownership strikes me deep, far beyond where he could reach.

"Mine," I say as he stills inside me.

But if all goes wrong…

For how long?

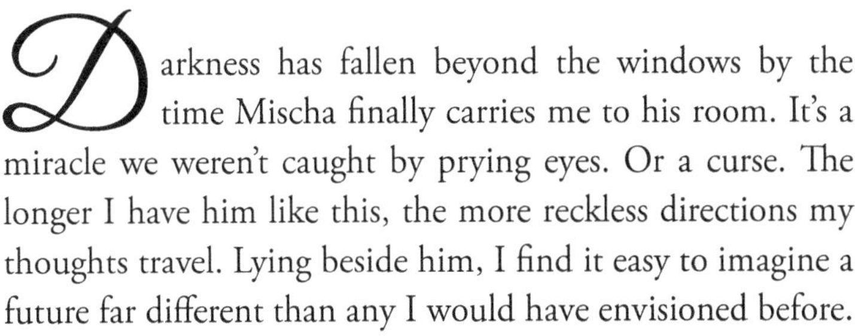

Darkness has fallen beyond the windows by the time Mischa finally carries me to his room. It's a miracle we weren't caught by prying eyes. Or a curse. The longer I have him like this, the more reckless directions my thoughts travel. Lying beside him, I find it easy to imagine a future far different than any I would have envisioned before.

A world where I'd live by his side and no one would dare intrude on our peace.

Strangely enough, I think he's imagining the same thing as he absently strokes my back. But there is no denying the reality waiting for us beyond these walls. We both stay stubbornly awake until a knock on the door draws him away.

"Vanya," he says, greeting the figure on the other side of the door.

"We're ready," the older man replies. "Everything is in place."

"Good." Mischa looks back at me and inclines his head.

Reluctantly, I creep from the mattress and redress beside him in the dark.

Together, he and Vanya descend the staircase while I follow. Sergei is waiting below, joined by several of his men.

"We should go now," he suggests as we approach. He's traded his posh suit from the meeting for a plain black sweater and slacks.

Frowning, Mischa inspects him and shrugs. "Fine. But first…"

He turns to me, and I stiffen as he reaches out, cupping my cheek. The brief affection isn't like him—especially with several startled eyes tracking his every movement. Oblivious to them, he tugs me in close, giving me no chance to resist as his lips boldly brush mine. At the same time, his hand slithers between us, unseen by the two men, and he presses something firm against my palm. My fingers automatically close around the shape and I tuck it behind my back as he deepens the kiss.

His teeth nip me, a brutal reminder of his prior warning: *Be on guard.* Gasping, I return the favor with a nipped message of my own: *I will.* Beneath my fingers, the item he gave me is easier to interpret. A weapon with a sturdy, leather handle.

"Ahem." As if from far away, Sergei clears his throat. "I don't mean to rush…"

"I'm ready." Mischa pulls back and heads for the door.

My cheeks flame as I catch Vanya staring, his gaze unreadable.

"Don't wait up, Little Rose," Mischa calls as the men approach the front door of the manor.

Sergei and Vanya flank him on either side while the rest take up the rear.

"Ellen?"

I turn and find Anna at the top of the stairs.

"Is everything all right?" Her wide eyes focus on the object I still have tucked behind my back. From this angle, only she can see it: a knife. It's too small to be Mischa's usual weapon but lethal enough, I suspect.

Facing her, I maneuver the object to keep it from sight. "Everything is fine." I smile even as my heart hammers in my chest.

For the first time, I look down and observe the knife fully. It's thinner than his blade and therefore easier for me to wield. That fact makes my stomach sink; he got it for me especially.

He planned for me to *need* it.

Or he could be giving in to his usual brand of paranoia. Yes. I nod along with the pathetic logic as Anna gapes at me from the top of the staircase. Everything, from his history lessons to his hostility toward Sergei, was a gross overreaction. If the former leader is right and they are able to capture Robert, then the meaning of the knife could be more subtle—a mocking reminder of everything I've sacrificed without Robert: blood, soul, limbs…

Even so, maybe I'm not ready to be a widow after all.

"You look like you've seen a ghost," Anna says as I finally ascend the stairs to her.

A ghost? Or a serpent. Sergei's soldier's tattoo reappears in my mind: a snake entwined with a cross. The more I think about it, the surer I am. He was the same man we saw the night we escaped from Robert.

"Ellen?"

When I meet Anna's gaze, I can tell she's worried. "I'll help you put the children to bed," I tell her, forcing a smile.

Together, we turn to the sitting room and usher a drowsy Mouse off to bed while Anna carries Eli.

At the threshold to her room, she grabs my arm. "Something's wrong, isn't it? I can see it in your face."

"No," I start to lie. Then I bite my lip and eye the blade in my grasp. "Keep an eye on him," I warn her, nodding to the boy sleeping against her shoulder. "And take this."

She stiffens when I press the blade against her palm, exposing it completely. "W-what is—"

"Hide it on you always," I insist, cutting her off. "And if anyone tries to take him… Use it."

"Who would take…" Suddenly, she swallows and then nods. "I understand."

⁂

I don't sleep. I stand and pace, wringing my hands together mercilessly. Around me, the old house creaks and sways, bustling with Sergei's men. Finally, after what must be midnight, I hear the sound of clamor coming from the foyer.

I race down the staircase, and Sergei is already at the bottom to meet me. Alarm lances through my chest as I spot the mud on his clothes. For once, ruffled hair and filthy hands ruin his usually polished façade.

But his bloodshot eyes stop me dead in my tracks, even before he says the words my brain takes ages to process.

"I'm sorry… But we failed."

"Oh," I croak. It's the only thing I seem capable of saying.

"Ellen…" Frowning, Sergei takes a step forward, his hand outstretched. "Mischa and Ivan…they're dead."

CHAPTER 25

I thought the day I lost my mother taught me what pain was. Even losing Eli the first time. My heart shattered, but I could still bear it and pull myself from the darkness.

I could make myself numb to reality and cushion myself within the bars of my cage.

But now…there is no more hiding and no shelter from the truth.

Even hearing it said out loud—the fact that Mischa could be gone—makes everything go black. When sensation returns, I'm on my knees, wrapped in the arms of someone whose silent sobs rack my body.

But I just stare blankly, eyeing a spot on the wall as Misha's voice echoes in my thoughts on a constant loop. *Be on guard. Be on guard.*

Don't trust him…

"I'm sorry," Sergei says, but something in his voice makes me bury my face into Anna's shoulder and obscure my expression from him. "We tried to recover the bodies, but it was too late. I'm sorry."

Anna continues to sob.

But I just listen. Mischa said that the night I went missing, Sergei put on a good show, but something was off. And I can hear it in his voice now.

He isn't gloating.

But he isn't devastated, either.

He's merely resigned.

And I feel that gnawing, consuming paranoia itching at my psyche, keeping true grief at bay.

He knows more than he's letting on.

And I can't fall apart now.

So, biting my lip, I lock the pain away. I keep the tears at bay, and I guard my heart against anything that might threaten its fragile surface.

Even if it kills a part of me.

*A*nna brings me to my room, her arms protectively around me. "Do you need me to stay with you?" she asks, choking her own sobs back. Blazing with concern, she scans my face and eases stray bits of hair from it. "I can—"

"No." I shake my head and turn from her, clinging to the door for balance. "Stay with Eli."

Once alone, I run my fingers along my face, surprised that there aren't any tears there to wipe away.

I wait long enough to hear Anna's steps retreat. Then I reenter the hall and descend the stairs. Unsurprisingly, I find Sergei alone in the drawing room, his back to me.

"What happened?" I demand hoarsely. "Tell me."

"It was an ambush." Turning to me, he sighs, raking his hands through his graying hair. "Winthorp must have anticipated our arrival. I did everything I could—"

"How did they die?"

He cocks his head at my tone, but finally, he unhooks his jaw. "We were separated," he says. "Unfortunately, when Robert's men retreated, I knew that—"

"That your man had done his job?"

"Ellen?" His eyes widen and narrow in rapid succession as my heart pounds a frantic rhythm against my rib cage. "I'm not sure I understand what you mean…"

"You let Robert take me." It sounds insane. I'm not even sure it's the truth—not until I see his expression harden. My heart solidifies into a throbbing, aching mass. Mischa was right. "Not for good," I add, still putting the pieces of my suspicion together. "You planned on retrieving me again. You had a man planted there and an easy route for him to enter my room via the vents—"

"And why would I do that?" he interjects, crossing his arms. The simple motion highlights just how large he is compared to me. A wall of muscle and power I have no chance at withstanding.

"Why?" I echo hollowly.

On the surface, such a plan makes little sense. But Mischa taught me well. I do what he would: view the situation from a different angle. I let my paranoia run rampant.

"Because I was never your true target," I blurt. "I'm still valuable to you, but one person could strengthen your position more than Robert's illegitimate wife. His son." My throat aches as I think of Eli, blissfully unaware of the games being played with him as a pawn. "You tried to bribe me into seeking him out myself. Maybe you would have revealed your plan then. But I refused. So you needed another method. For whatever reason, you knew that Robert would keep me near him. I just don't understand why."

"Why?" He faces me directly, his mouth thoughtfully tilted. "He's an easy man to manipulate—once you understand him."

"Robert?" I risk venturing a guess. "I think your goal was always to get control of Eli."

"He's the heir," he says simply. "Without him, Robert can't shore up support. Eventually, his empire will crumble around his fucking hands—"

"Then why didn't you say something!" My voice rings out, bleating and broken. It's a weakness. One I desperately try to regain control of, choking any hint of tears back. "Why all the secrecy and the lies?"

"And concede it all to Mischa?"

I jump as he advances toward me and brushes his hand along my cheek. Stripped of any feigned gentleness, his touch burns: callused flesh and brute strength.

"Mischa, the impulsive, violent fool who would run this enterprise into the ground?"

"You killed him." I fight any lingering tears back and force myself to meet his stare. This is the one truth I won't let him avoid. "Didn't you?"

"No." He sighs. Disappointed in that fact? "I didn't. But he is dead. I can assure you of that."

"And Vanya?" Again, my voice breaks. Gasping for air, I can't disguise the pain in it any longer. "Mischa was your rival, fine. But your own brother?"

"Ivan was an accident," he admits, turning his back to me. Even so, guilt radiates from his hunched posture—which only confuses me further.

"An accident?"

"Yes! Don't look at me with hate in your eyes," he snaps. "I loved him, even when he betrayed me. I was the only person who ever looked after him."

"Like with my mother?"

He should laugh at the insinuation. It's too petty to even consider. But he shoots me a look that chills my blood. It gleams with the malice he managed to conceal until now.

And I can easily discern the truth.

"You lied to him about her," I whisper in horror. "Didn't you?"

"Your mother..." He laughs darkly, failing to hide the loathing in his voice. "She was a haughty little bitch. She had Ivan wrapped around her finger. She put ideas into his head. Made him question what he shouldn't."

"Like you," I surmise. "She didn't trust you."

"No." His mouth flattens into a thoughtful line. "I suppose she didn't. Ever since I ordered my men to leave her precious whelp behind."

He says it so coldly that one could miss the true cruelty implied.

"Briar." I fight to keep the disgust from my tone. "You used her as a bargaining chip. Didn't you?"

On paper, he had a powerful weapon against the Winthorps in the form of Marnie to use against Robert Sr.

But he still needed leverage to control the woman herself.

And a mother would do anything for her child.

Even if it cost her the man she loved.

"I don't think Ivan ever believed her suspicions." He frowns and then shakes his head. "No. He would have killed me if he knew. But Marnie grew more devious. The time came when I knew she would run off with him and my—the Winthorp money."

"So you tricked her," I say. "Vanya thought she went back willingly, but that wasn't the case."

He nods as if finally admitting it all is freeing to him. Cathartic. "I promised her Briar. Then I told Ivan she left." The wry twist to his mouth could be guilt. Or smug satisfaction. "It broke his heart, but it had to be done—"

"All so that you could maintain power."

"For the good of the Vasilev name," he growls, his voice booming. "Ivan was too worried about sticking his cock in a pretty woman and siring more children. But *I* had the mantle of the *mafiya* on my shoulders. I had our family name on my shoulders—"

"But you abandoned your own family," I hiss. "She told you about me. Didn't she?"

"She tried to reach Ivan," he says. "I managed to intercept her messages, though I don't think she realized that. She pleaded for him to come for her. Then she primarily pleaded for you. In her words, even if he didn't love her…" He laughs again. "She begged him to take you."

My eyes burn, watering as I imagine Marnie. Her face. The pained way she looked at me. How she held me the few times she could. My pathetic, faithfully acknowledged birthdays…

All this time, I thought I was the source of her pain—but I wasn't.

Her heart broke for *me*.

"You made her think Vanya abandoned her," I say thickly. "And you left her to rot."

"I did what was best for Ivan." But from the grit in his tone, I doubt he believes that lie himself. "The fool would have gotten himself killed. Besides, he had Anna-Natalia—"

"Until she was taken," I point out. "But rather than rescuing her, you went after a child." A sudden thought churns my stomach. "Was hurting Marnie your real intention for wanting to kill Briar? Punishing her?"

"Are you really that naïve?" His eyes flicker and I instinctively take a step back. For the first time, the true Sergei Vasilev peeks from beneath his charming mask. Not a vengeful brute like Mischa, but something far more dangerous.

A cold, calculating tactician content to wait years to see his plans bear fruit.

No matter the cost.

"We spun Marnie's little excursion to our own benefit, but Winthorp retaliated much harder than I expected. I'm sure Mischa told you about what happened to his family? Imagine countless more gruesome tales, and widows, and pain. Not to mention what we thought happened to Anna."

"You saw my mother that night, didn't you?"

"I did," he says. "And knowing what I do now, I should have spit in her face."

"You're a monster! She learned better than to trust you. In her eyes, Anna was better locked in a Winthorp dungeon than anywhere near you—"

I don't even see the slap; it happens so fast. Then I blink, realizing I'm on my knees and Sergei is standing above me.

"I see you are like your mother in more ways than one. Eric!" He raises his voice and a man appears in the doorway. The one with the serpent tattoo. "Miss Winthorp is tired," Sergei says, waving a dismissive hand in my direction. "Please show her to her room."

The man approaches me and grabs my arm, hauling me to my feet. As he steers me to the door, I look back at Sergei. "Are you going to give me back to Robert?"

It's my obvious fate: With Eli under his control, he no longer needs me.

"No," he says. "But I will *sell* you back to him. Long enough to serve as a distraction while I put the pieces into play to obliterate his standing completely. Mischa wasn't as stupid as he pretended to be, but he was a fool," Sergei says. "He didn't realize that men like the Winthorps can't simply be butchered out of existence. With their money and prestige, it takes a slow, methodical approach to ensure their demise. I need to infest his holdings from the inside out and crumble the house of cards from the very foundation."

In some ways, it's a more gruesome end for Robert than a bullet would be.

"So what now?"

For a second, I think he won't tell me as his man drags me over the threshold. Then he holds his hand up and the man stops.

"I'll tell him that Mischa flew into a rage and killed the boy. I can offer you to him—for a price. And while he enjoys you in your current condition, I will solidify my alliances and then burn the manor to the ground when he least expects it."

Presumably with both Robert and me inside it.

Swallowing hard, I ask, "And Eli?"

"I'll ensure that he remains the sole inheritor of the Winthorp estate," he says. "Then I'll train the boy to take his rightful place as my successor. Maybe that will give you solace. He'll learn the Vasilev way, just as I did. Goodnight, Ellen."

The man, Eric, ushers me up the stairs and into my room. Once the door closes, I hear the lock engage.

And I can't help wondering if, before he sent her back to the Winthorps, Sergei made this room my mother's prison as well.

CHAPTER 26

Robert was a cruel captor and Mischa a ruthless one—but Sergei is methodical. When my door opens in the morning, his man enters and places a tray of food on my nightstand.

It's not a bowl of gruel or the stale bread of a prisoner's rations. Though the scrambled eggs and porridge could easily contain a lethal powder. So could the orange juice or the steaming mug of tea.

Maybe he wants me to suspect as much. A part of me bristles at the paranoia.

But even Mischa let his guard down around Sergei.

I can't afford a single mistake.

So I ignore the tray and sit on the bed with my back to it. Closing my eyes, I think.

If Mischa were here, what plan would he compile? Something reckless and violent, no doubt. Though maybe that's the only way to counter methodical planning—brute strength.

Had I his knife, he'd probably urge me to stab the next person to bring me a meal. Stab Sergei afterward. Run.

But I know, even as I let the fantasy play in my mind, that my method needs to be different. Desperation is what Sergei expects. As Mischa claimed, a man like him is already one move away from checkmate.

The only way to beat such a foe?

Play a different game.

As my mind parses over every potential escape, I barely hear the door open.

"You haven't eaten," Sergei remarks with feigned surprise. "Maybe you'll find your lunch more palatable?"

Ignoring him, I eye the wall as he replaces the trays, and finally, he leaves. Newer smells tickle my nose in his wake. Soup? It's no matter. I close my eyes and focus on a game— but one far simpler than the elaborate chess match I grew up in.

The same one I can hear Mouse and Eli playing right now, innocent of everything else.

Cat and mouse.

And the most effective chases require only bait.

And sheer desperation.

263

When the tattooed man returns with my dinner tray, I stand and face him.

"Take me to Sergei," I command, meeting his startled gaze directly. "Now."

He frowns, but I suspect that Sergei warned him that I might make such a request. Without hesitation, he turns and beckons with a jerk of his chin. "Come but stay close."

And don't you dare run.

I follow him down the hall and nearly sigh with relief when we pass the sitting room. As if conjured by a miracle, Anna, Mouse, and Eli are already inside it.

"Ellen?" Anna lurches to her feet. Her eyes dart to the man in the hall, but there's a grim resignation in her gaze. Years with the Winthorps haven't made her naïve. "Are you all right?"

"I'm fine." I force a smile. "Mouse?"

The girl sits hunched on the floor beside Eli. I don't doubt she's already picked up on the inevitable shift in the atmosphere as well. Her eyes are sharp as they meet mine, as guarded as always.

Still smiling, I make my voice deliberately soft. "You and Eli should play a game. Remember the one you and Mischa played?" I pray to God that she understands. "This time, he is the flower." I point to Eli, who wrinkles his nose.

"I don't want to be a flower—"

"Hush, darling," Anna scolds. She tracks the silent communication between me and the girl, biting her lower lip.

"Wouldn't that be fun, Mouse?" I say, hoping the fear isn't apparent in my voice. "A game?"

With her as silent as always, I can't gauge her reaction. It's like Mischa gave her lessons in masking her emotions as well as knife fighting. Finally, she nods.

"Come, miss," the man prods. His hand brushes my lower back—a warning.

Reluctantly, I follow him down the stairs and across the foyer. Instead of the drawing room, he leads me to a different space, closer to the staircase: a study. Inside it, Sergei is sitting behind a desk, studiously eyeing a pile of documents.

"Can I help you, Ellen?" he wonders without looking up.

"I wanted to know when you were sending me back," I demand. "Because you are, aren't you?"

"What an odd coincidence." He shuffles his papers and finally looks up. "I was just about to make the arrangements. You'll return to your husband tonight. I was merely waiting for confirmation."

My stomach sinks at his cold, mocking tone. "C-confirmation?"

He slides something across the desk toward me. My eyes process the item in pieces: silver blade. Leather handle.

It's a knife, long and battered. Recognition shreds my heart. It's *Mischa's* knife. Only now, blood streaks the surface its owner strived so hard to polish.

"No..." My breath catches on a moan as I sink to my knees. At the back of my mind, I never believed he was dead.

But this...

Logic goes to war with blind faith, utilizing my heart as their battlefield.

Alive.

Dead.

Alive.

Dead...

"That is one matter of business handled," Sergei says. His callous tone is a harsh anchor, grounding me amid the wave of grief threatening to drown me.

I can't lose focus now, and Mischa's old mantra returns to haunt me. *Breathe!* I inhale raggedly, and through a screen of tears, I watch Sergei stand and rummage through a drawer.

"Now for the other." He looks at the man behind me. "Retrieve the boy—"

"No!" I lunge to my feet, but I barely go a step before a hand latches onto my arm from behind, locking me in place. "No! Don't you dare touch him!"

Oblivious to me, the tattooed man ascends the stairs. Seconds later, he returns—but my knees buckle with relief.

He's alone. He doesn't have Eli.

"The woman said they are 'playing'," he tells Sergei.

I fight to smother any reaction I might reveal, despite how my heart hammers. Mouse listened. I can only pray that she can stay out of sight long enough.

"Playing?" Sergei wrenches me around to face him. Whatever he sees makes him grunt in appreciation. "Make sure he's found."

"What do you want with him?" I risk asking. "He's a child. He's too young to inherit anything regardless—"

"Is that so?" His jaw clenches. He doesn't want to tell me, and I half expect another slap. But he sighs. "By tomorrow, I'll have him in Moldova, nestled away in a family compound—"

"Why?" I place my hand on his shoulder imploringly. "Why not let him stay with me? His mother—"

"Why?" He smooths his hand along my cheek. "And let you plant foolish ideas in his head?"

Pain bites into my jaw as his nails flex against the skin, robbing any kindness from the gesture.

"So that you can mold him the way you've twisted Mischa—"

"Let go of me!" I cringe out of his reach. "Don't touch me!"

He releases me so suddenly that I trip and fall to my knees. Then he sinks into a crouch and meets my gaze. "You haven't asked, but I know you've considered it: How could I let you go back if you could easily tell Robert all you know?" He raises a brown bottle that I didn't realize was in his grasp and shakes it. "Mischa has an associate who likes to use unwitting innocents as drug mules. To keep them silent, he had some unethical physicians concoct a poison that paralyzes the vocal cords, rendering the victim unable to speak." He cuts his gaze to Eric. "Hold her."

The man grabs me from behind. I struggle, but it's no use. Together, the men pry my lips apart and Sergei pours the liquid down. It's bitter, like copper. Or blood.

The second it hits my tongue, I put all my energy into choking, spitting out every drop.

"Swallow," Sergei demands. His hand encircles my throat, squeezing until my eyes water. When he finally releases me, I instinctively swallow, gasping for air.

Fire sears down my esophagus. Any noise I make comes out hoarse and broken.

It's like he struck a match inside me and chased it with gasoline.

"Get her in the van," Sergei commands loudly enough to rise above my wheezing.

The man grabs me, dragging me to my feet. My eyes stream as he ushers me from the manor and unceremoniously shoves me into the enclosed space minutes later. I scramble to get my bearings and reach for the door, but it's already locked. I'm in the back. I feel around for an emergency lever or anything I can use as a weapon, but I find nothing.

Seconds later, the van begins to move, pitching me forward. To protect myself as much as possible, I curl into a ball and try to steady my breathing. My only hope is that Mouse got Eli away. Just long enough…

For what?

It terrifies me that I didn't think that far ahead.

But now…

I have to find my own way to keep them safe. Even if it means dropping to my knees before Robert. Even if it means selling my soul in the process.

I'll do whatever desperate, dirty thing required to prevent Sergei from getting the upper hand.

But in the meantime, he has the last laugh; all I can do at the moment is suffer and wait.

We must travel for hours. By the time the van finally stops, I can't tell how far we are from Sergei's property. It's still dark out. In the early morning hours, I'm guessing. As the door opens from the outside, I tense.

"Come on." The man, Eric, grabs me and drags me from the van before I have a prayer of mounting an attack.

I blink to make out our surroundings as a gravel-like substance irritates the soles of my bare feet. The moon illuminates snatches of bushes and looming shadows—but a familiar stench makes my heart lurch. Fresh roses.

Like the kind that bloom on Winthorp manor.

Before I can be sure, Eric unfurls a strip of cloth from his pocket and wraps it around my eyes, snagging pieces of my hair in the process. Then he shoves me forward over uneven terrain that quickly gives way to a smooth, firm surface.

The air here feels thinner. Colder. A basement or garage?

"Be careful with her," a chillingly familiar voice commands from up ahead. "That's close enough for you. Let her go."

Grunting, Eric releases me, and I hear his footsteps echo as he retreats.

I'm left shaking, tears welling behind my blindfold. My body quakes down to my core, resisting the confines of my old cage as the doors to it figuratively slam shut. I'll never escape before it's too late. Eli and Mouse are already recaptured. So much for my so-called teaching. I'm just a pathetic doe, always on the run. I'm trapped. Forever…

Enough. Gritting my teeth, I bite any sobs back as heavy footsteps approach me. The time for self-pity is over.

Mouse.

Eli.

They consume my concern. To save them, I'll do anything.

Even if it means placating Robert. He's the one approaching me, his steps unsteady over what I sense is concrete flooring.

"Elle…" Soft fingers swipe at my cheek in their search for my blindfold, undoing the knot—but that's as much as he'll allow himself to touch me. "Are you hurt?" Robert scans me from head to toe. His finger hesitates near the corner of my mouth.

Licking the area, I taste blood.

"She's bleeding," he says before swallowing in distaste. Anger distorts his expression, and my heart pangs as I catch the subtle resemblance between him and Eli. They both can't hide their emotions for long, and now? Robert is murderous. "You bastards will pay—"

"R…" I try to speak. "Rob—"

"Sir!" A louder, masculine voice cuts me off. A man dressed in a black suit brushes past me and leans toward Robert, murmuring something into his ear.

"Damn it," Robert hisses, his hands clenching into fists. "Put her with the other one. They won't look for her there."

Before I can react, the blindfold is drawn over my eyes a second time.

"This way, miss." Someone grabs my arm and steers me in a different direction.

I strain my ears, desperate to track any other figures nearby or any clue as to my surroundings.

"Mr. Winthorp will see you shortly," the man adds. "You'll be home soon enough."

Home?

Rather than elaborate, the man leads me forward until he comes to an abrupt stop. I stiffen as he tugs at my blindfold, removing it. Frantically, I blink to make my vision come into focus: vast darkness. A heartbeat later, a door closes behind me.

I'm in a room. That much I can tell.

I feel along the nearest wall in search of a light switch. Despite flicking it, no light comes on. Eventually, I wind up sinking onto a carpeted floor with my back to the wall.

Only now do I realize I'm not alone. A slender figure creeps through the darkness toward me.

I stiffen, but they're too slight to do much damage, almost as tiny as Mouse.

"Hello?" a woman whispers, her voice familiar.

The closer she comes, the more of her I can clearly make out as cold recognition robs me of any urgency for a precious few seconds. Bright, familiar curls drape her shoulders. Her pale skin gleams in the darkness, and her huge blue eyes glisten like mirrors, reflecting my own terror back at me.

"Ellen?" Briar whispers. Her hand brushes my shoulder and she jerks it back as if burned. "Is that you?"

I can't speak, though my throat isn't the cause. In a relatively short amount of time, I've gone through so many wild emotions when it comes to my sister. Nearly twenty-four years of devotion have been reduced to a grim uncertainty.

Did I ever really know her?

Did she ever even love me?

All this time, I thought I was Marnie's dirty little secret she hid in shame. Now, I know the truth—she loved me enough to risk her life for me, countless times.

And she loved Briar enough to gamble her freedom.

And ultimately forfeit it.

"I don't know what's happening," my sister whispers, demanding my attention. "I don't…" She breaks off, her mouth flat. "I know you hate me. I… You don't understand what it's like. The wedding, and Father, and—none of this was supposed to happen!" Her voice shakes. "When Robert volunteered to lead the wedding procession to the airport, I knew." She laughs bitterly, shaking her head. "I knew there was a reason. But I didn't… I just thought if he were planning something, he'd get a big fucking shock if I outsmarted him for once. I didn't think you'd be hurt." She runs her fingers along her uninjured cheek. "Or maybe I did. Maybe I knew something bad would happen and I wanted you gone."

Hearing her admit as much out loud stings—far worse than I could have anticipated. Old wounds sear over my psyche: that constant fear of being unwanted. Of never fitting in.

Of being a burden.

Despite everything, I risk irritating the sore flesh of my throat to ask, "Why?"

She shrugs. "I spent my entire goddamn life being compared to you. Perfect Ellen. Sweet Ellen. Servants. Friends. Robert…even Mother loved you more. Maybe I wanted to know what it would finally be like if you were gone and I was just Briar without the more appealing shadow."

She sounds so young. So…desperate. Any hatred or resentment I may have felt disintegrates. Now? I only feel pity.

"Ellen, please say something!"

In silence, I reach for her hand, curling my fingers around her thin, trembling ones. Then I lean my head against the wall, close my eyes, and try to gather my strength.

Because this war isn't over yet.

It hasn't even started.

*M*ouse. *Eli. Mouse. Eli.* It's the only mantra I have left worth clinging to. *Mouse. Eli…*

Faint thuds jar me from my reverie and I stiffen, lurching into a crouch.

"What's that?" Beside me, Briar scrambles to her feet. "Something's happening," she whispers, dragging me upright as well. "Did you hear that? I think the guard is leaving! I don't know what's going on."

But I do. Distant shouts allude to only one kind of danger.

Sergei.

Damn. I start searching the room, cursing myself for not having done so sooner. How could I be so damn pathetic? No matter, the time for self-pity is over. There's a window in the corner of the room. I scramble toward it and attempt to open it.

"It's locked," Briar whispers, creeping to my side. "There're guards nearby too—"

I turn away from her and stop at a sideboard table. There's nothing on it but a lace doily and a vase—a metal statue. I grab it, pushing any doubting thoughts back. Then I turn to the window and slam it against the glass with all my might.

Glass rains down with an alarming crack as it gives way. Heedless of the pain, I knock away any loose shards, creating an opening barely large enough to slip through. Warm liquid drips between my fingers, but I ignore it.

"Come," I croak to Briar. God, speaking even that little hurts. Despite everything, a vain voice inside me wonders if the damage is permanent.

How ironic: I find my voice, only to die silenced.

"What now?" Briar asks, eyeing the makeshift opening.

I grit my teeth, grounding myself to the present. Now? If we're lucky, the guards aren't already on their way.

We're on a lower level, I realize with a sense of relief that nearly barrels me over. A carefully manicured terrain stretches out: flower beds, and paddocks, and enclosed paths. Even in the dark, I recognize it: the west gardens. Meaning we must be imprisoned at, of all places, the guesthouse.

Of Winthorp Manor.

"What now?" Briar asks again.

"Climb," I croak, shoving her forward.

"Ow!" She whines, struggling to maneuver her limbs through the opening. Finally, she disappears and her soft groan alludes to the fact that she made it safely below.

I scramble after her, feet first. Glass bites deep, and more alarmingly, hot liquid coats my limbs. When I let go of the sill, I grunt, landing hard on an earthen surface. Bolting upright, I grab Briar's hand and run, heading toward the back of the property.

But we're already too late.

Briar screams as a smattering of gunshots pierce the air dangerously close. Once again, Sergei lied to me; he won't even give Robert the chance to enjoy our little reunion.

He'll kill us all first.

"What's going on?" Briar squeals.

It's a good question. From this part of the estate, the only way forward cuts through the expansive gardens between the guesthouse and main manor. The whole damn manor could be on fire for all we know.

Heading there at all would be foolish.

But it's the only way out. From the garage, I could steal a car or a van and find my way back to Sergei's manor. I could find Mouse and Eli on my own.

Deep down, I know it's a stupid, foolish plan.

But I spent sixteen years living my life in the safest way I knew.

"We need to hide!" Briar rasps. "This way—"

She tugs me toward the farthest gardens, but I break away.

"Ellen!"

"Hide," I hiss to her. Then, shrugging aside her attempts to pull me back, I take off toward the main manor.

Idiot! I imagine Mischa shouting. *Hide!* Running toward danger is the stupidest thing I've done.

Reckless.

Selfish.

But, in war, there are no true winners. Here, in the sanctity of the Winthorp stronghold, Sergei has the advantage.

And he can't win.

My breaths rip from me as I run, plowing my bare feet over the cool grass. It's surreal in a sense, being inside my old cage as it's attacked from within. The beautifully tended flowerbeds of Winthorp manor create a mocking backdrop to the figures, dressed in black, streaming across it, wielding weapons.

Mischa made his name through his combat prowess—but Sergei can apparently muster the same amount of manpower.

He hasn't brought just one henchman to ensure his victory —he brought an army.

They cut boldly through the heart of the property, heedless of any Winthorp men who may be out on patrol.

I stick to the outskirts. Up ahead, the breathtaking façade of my childhood home stands, bathed in moonlight. The fighting started here, it seems.

Breaking glass and more gunshots allude to the battle raging within.

And every fiber of my being warns me to run. Hide. My heart pounds as I search for clarity among the shadowy figures battling on the terrace. I see nothing but sparks as guns fire and glass shatters.

I have to keep moving. As the clamor and violence rage around me, I deafen myself to everything but the sound of my ragged breathing. Then I set my sights on the detached building housing all Winthorp vehicles and inch my way toward it.

Mouse. Eli. Mouse. Eli...

"Ellen!" Someone grabs my arm, spinning me around.

A scream crawls up my throat before I even make out my captor's face, gleaming in the moonlit dark. I was so focused on the garage that I didn't even realize I'd passed the west end of the Manor entirely.

Here, it seems, Robert and a contingent of bodyguards have made their last stand. Fitting, since they create a makeshift barricade before the guesthouse and the prisoners he had locked inside it.

"What are you doing out here?" Robert demands. He cuts his gaze to a uniformed guard standing beside him, his face white with rage. "It's no fucking matter now." He grabs my arm, dragging me forward as he approaches a black van, flanked by two more bodyguards. "I'll keep you safe," he swears. "Once we're away from this fucking place, I'll never let you—"

He breaks off, his eyes wide, staring blankly ahead. His lips move, but no words come from them.

Just blood. Splatters of it speckle my cheek as he goes limp and falls backward, his mouth frozen in a startled O.

I can't scream.

Can't breathe.

In an array of beautiful, terrible noise, several quiet pops echo one by one, and the rest of the men around me go down in the same way.

Shot.

Dazed, I turn around in time to catch the killer, aiming his weapon at me. He's alone—I register that first as my brain tracks his approach in slow motion. His gray hair catches fire in the moonlight, making him seem more ethereal than human. A demon, his teeth bared in rage.

Panting, he says something my brain can't process and then aims the gun directly over my heart.

"Ellen, look out!"

Blond hair gleams in the air as a slender figure dashes from the front of the manor. Briar. Startled, Sergei turns toward her and the world explodes with a monstrous sound. *Bang!*

Acrid smoke tickles my throat as my ears ring in the aftermath. I can taste death; it comes *that* close to claiming me. But, as I stagger a few steps back, I realize I'm unscathed.

He missed…

But I wasn't his target. Paces away, a limp, blonde figure lies motionless on the lawn.

"No!" Even as I scream, there isn't time to think. React. Mourn.

Sergei's already whirling in my direction—but he doesn't expect the second I lunge.

There's no way I can overpower him. Stunning him is my only goal as my hand grapples with his. The gun swishes wildly in his grasp, pointing at me. The ground.

"Shit!" Finally, he drops it entirely.

But I don't have long to feel triumphant.

"You bitch!" He grabs my throat, wrenching my feet off the ground.

In vain, I strain and kick and flail until he trips, crushing me to the ground. Panic flares as the air leaves my chest. I brace my hand protectively over my stomach and fight for leverage to slip from his grasp.

"You little bitch," he grunts, tightening his grip. "I knew the moment I saw you that you were like her," he hisses. "Marnie Winthorp. Meddling and foolish—"

"I…saw…through you," I manage to croak. "Just…like… she did…"

Blood rushes through my ears, drowning him out. Closing my eyes, I focus every ounce of strength I have into kicking. Clawing. Biting. But he's no easy foe to overpower.

His angry growls seep into my ears as every attempt I make to resist has less and less impact. "Just…like….that fucking…whore…"

Suddenly, he stiffens, impossibly heavy. Crushing me…

"Ellen?"

The faint shout triggers a sharp pang through my chest. Hope? I open my eyes as unseen hands roll Sergei off of me. Gasping for breath, I blink up at the figure in question, braced to fight. A haggard face stares back at me and I shake my head. I'm dreaming.

Still, I indulge my insanity. "V-Vanya?"

He's holding a knife. Blood streaks the tip and my brain takes a pathetically long second to put the pieces together: the weapon, the unmistakable shape of a larger body lying beside mine.

Swallowing hard, Vanya flexes his free hand without looking away from me once. "Come with me." He hauls me to my feet, and into his arms.

"Briar…"

"She's alive." He jerks his chin toward a man racing past us, Briar in his arms.

But she wasn't the only potential victim.

I crane my neck, hunting for the awkward shape lying on the ground nearby. "Sergei—"

"Don't look." Vanya grabs my chin, forcing me to face him. "Come. Come!"

"How?" I rasp as he approaches the main manor. "How?"

It isn't long before someone lunges from the dark to meet us and I have my answer.

A tattered scream rips from my throat. First, from fear. Then, as the moonlight plays over the planes of the attacker's face…

Air wheezes from my chest as any words I mean to say die as a gasp. I'm dreaming. I have to be. But even my imagination isn't so vivid.

I could never recreate the grated cadence of his voice.

"You're shaking, Little Rose," he scolds as I scramble from Vanya's grasp.

I'm falling. My knees give way, but he catches me, looping an arm around my shoulders. "Mischa—"

"Did he hurt you?" he asks near my ear. "If he touched you, I swear to God, I'll kill him."

I shake my head, hoping it conveys my meaning: I don't matter. Inhaling deeply, I try to speak. "He has…" My voice is a thin, broken mockery, barely discernable.

"It's all right," Mischa snaps. He angles my face toward him and I can't stop myself from tracing the rugged features.

My hands shake so badly that my nails catch his flesh. I have to be hurting him, but he doesn't so much as flinch.

He doesn't fade away beneath my fingertips, at least. His heat is a cushion against the chill encasing me. I can feel his heart hammering through his rib cage, as his arms cradle me, firm and gentle all at once.

"You're dead," I whisper, cringing with the pain it takes to say even that little. "Dead—"

"I would be," he says softly, for my ears only. "If it wasn't for your friend Somodorov." He chuckles as my eyes widen in shock. Gingerly, his thumb teases the corner of my mouth. "Apparently, a certain whore made him rethink his alliances. He intervened during Sergei's ambush—"

"Mischa," Vanya calls. "We need to move. Now."

"Mouse and Eli," I say, forcing the words from my raw throat. "We need—"

"They're safe," he says. "We went there first, but you were already gone. Mouse had him hidden." He laughs gruffly, shaking his head. "I almost didn't fucking find them. But then we came for you."

Which is why Sergei had to move up his timeline by attacking so soon.

"Mischa!" Vanya jerks his chin toward a van idling in the main courtyard. "We need to move."

Mischa grits his teeth. "Sergei still has his allies," he says as he hastens me toward the van.

From the pain in his tone, I know that his worst fear is now a reality.

The *mafiya* has split down the middle.

And we've just ushered in a new war.

***

"We're here," Mischa says into my ear.

Dazed, I blink my eyes open and my heart jolts in my chest. Of all the places to find looming beyond the van, Sergei's manor wasn't on my list.

"It's safe," Mischa says as I stiffen. "We drove off his men. No one else would dare attack it now—"

"It's *my* home," Vanya says gruffly from the front seat. Reaching back, he grabs my hand and squeezes reassuringly.

"Even those loyal to Sergei wouldn't dare strike here. Not if they want to keep breathing."

The coldness in his tone bolsters the threat and I have no doubt he'd follow through. I'm not sure how much of Sergei's rant he overheard, but something in his gaze is different. Harder. Pained.

Maybe I'm selfish for wanting to ease it the only way I know how.

"She…loved you," I rasp as Mischa exits the van and pulls me into his arms. "My mother. She—"

"I know," Vanya says hoarsely, his eyes downcast. His hands are in fists, the knuckles stark white against his tanned, callused skin. "I know."

Mischa pulls me away before I can say anything else. This conversation will have to be continued later.

"Stay with me, Little Rose," he warns, his voice rumbling in his chest. "Don't you dare close your eyes. Stay with me."

He's not worried about any life-threatening injuries, I suspect.

For once, Mischa Stepanov is more direct than anything else.

Stay with him.

Without Robert.

Despite the end of the Winthorp war.

Despite the *mafiya*.

Stay with him, in spite of the targets on all of our backs.

Trust in him….

But not for survival, or security, or any other lies I could feed myself.

Stay with him because I want to, even if it means fighting for every scrap of peace.

Even if it means never finding it at all.

EPILOGUE

My mother was wrong. Hell isn't a rose. Hell is love. The agony of blind desire. Trust in the face of inevitable destruction. The acceptance of death to protect the breath of another.

Even so, under all the violence, it's undeniably beautiful.

In lieu of fire and brimstone, my Hades contains a small garden overflowing with roses. A gothic manor serves as its austere backdrop, but just a few weeks of childish laughter have eased the darkness lurking in its shadows.

A beautiful blond boy runs screaming through the gardens, chased by a silent girl with golden hair.

And my devil stands beside me, frowning at the display. "What are you doing?" he bellows. "Run her down!"

Heeding his advice, Eli changes tack, tackling Mouse to the ground.

"More military games?" I ask, raising an eyebrow. "Anna will kill you if Eli winds up with another bruise, you know."

"They need to learn," he counters. "One day, he might be thankful for surviving a battle with *just* a bruise."

I sigh internally at the reminder. Sergei's death created a void several of his allies have jockeyed to fill. There have been no outright attacks—yet. But the prospect keeps Mischa up at night and worry has deepened the lines around his mouth. Just as the thought crosses my mind, he spites me by flashing a wicked grin.

"Besides…the piano lessons start Tuesday."

"You're not serious." As I gape, the line of his mouth softens, just a fraction of an inch.

Even now, nearly a month after Robert's death, he gives me only snippets of what lurks beneath his mask. Just enough to reassure myself that this demonic creature is still human.

"I don't know… Maybe they should be able to play music before stabbing the first bastard to piss them off? My children won't be pampered runts," he adds, his tone harsh. "But table manners couldn't hurt, either."

"*Your* children?" My throat rasps.

Turning away from me, he steps forward, drawing Eli and Mouse's attention. "You." He jabs a finger at Eli and the boy startles to a stop, blinking. "And you." He nods toward Mouse. "Do you think you have what it takes to be Stepanovs?"

The two share a look and then nod solemnly in unison.

"Good. You." Again, he points to Eli. Then he moves toward a nearby rose bush and plucks a blooming rose from a stem. He rips a petal from it and then sinks to one knee, pressing the petal against Eli's forehead. "You are now Eli Mischovich Stepanov."

The boy watches him with all the reverence of a knight being anointed by a king.

"As for you." He beckons Mouse closer, frowning. "You need a real name. Will you tell me yours?"

She eyes him and then shakes her head, and I can't help wondering about her past. Despite the chaos, Mischa went to Nicolai about her, demanding answers, but all the man could tell him was that she had been sold to him.

Sold by a man named Donatello Vanici.

I'm not brave enough to wonder what she endured before then—and I can't blame her for not wanting a reminder.

If it weren't for Eli, I'm not sure I'd ever want to be reminded of the creature I used to be, either. Even Briar seemed too ashamed to face our shared past. Not long after we regrouped here at Vasilev Manor, she disappeared. So did one of the few Winthorp soldiers to survive Sergei's assault and defect to Mischa's *mafiya*. Maybe, in her own way, she thought we were even.

I saved her life years ago.

She saved mine.

"What about a new name?" I suggest.

"Something better than Mouse," Mischa seconds, ruffling her hair.

The girl wrinkles her nose. Then she points to one of the trees at the back of the property.

"Tree?" Mischa asks, incredulous.

"Willow?" I say, making a guess of my own.

Smiling, she nods.

"Fine. Willow it is." Mischa rips another petal from the rose in his hand and presses it to her forehead. "Willow Mischovna Stepanova."

"What about this one?" I ask, stepping forward. My hand cradles my belly and Mischa promptly sinks to one knee, pressing a petal against my abdomen.

"This one…" He frowns, mulling it over. "Mischa Junior."

A laugh escapes me. "And if it's a girl?"

He shrugs. "Mischa Junior."

I roll my eyes as he stands, drawing me close. His lips flutter over my cheek, imparting a million promises he can't say out loud.

Danger swirls around us—maybe it always will.

But, this time, we'll face it, two wolves with nothing to fear.

Side by side.

Hey there!

Thank you so much for reading! If you enjoyed the story, please leave a review and recommend the book to any friend you think would love this twisted world. You'd have my eternal gratitude. Even a short sentence goes a long way!

Then, come join the rest of us dark romance lovers in my Facebook Group where you can get snippets, sneak peeks of upcoming books and even help vote on aspects of future novels.

Come to the dark side:

https://www.facebook.com/groups/lanasbeautifulmonsters/

WANT MORE STUFF TO READ?

Join my newsletter and get a **free book**! Plus, you get to stay updated with any new releases, random giveaways and exclusive sneak peeks!

https://www.lanaskybooks.com/newsletter

Lana Sky is a reclusive writer in the United States who spends most of her time daydreaming about complex male characters and parenting her Cockapoo Joey. She writes dark, twisted romance across several genres. Her titles include everything from mafia romance to vampires.

facebook.com/AuthorLanaSky

twitter.com/lanasky101

amazon.com/author/lanasky

pinterest.com/lanasky101

goodreads.com/lanasky

instagram.com/lanasky101

bookbub.com/authors/lana-sky

www.ingramcontent.com/pod-product-compliance
Lightning Source LLC
Chambersburg PA
CBHW071728190726
48292CB00003B/660